THINGS TO MAKE
AND BREAK

May-Lan Tan

The author is grateful to her mother and her father and to Siu-Lan Tan, Danny Kim, David Riding, Michael Ray, Paul Bush, and Gordon Lish.

First published in 2014
by CB editions
146 Percy Road London W12 9QL
www.cbeditions.com

Reprinted 2014

"Legendary" first appeared in *Zoetrope: All-Story*,
"DD-MM-YY" in *Areté*, and "101" in *The Reader*.

Printed in England by Blissetts, London W3 8DH

ISBN 978–1–909585-01-0

For Mikołaj

THINGS TO MAKE AND BREAK

May-Lan Tan grew up in Hong Kong, where her family had migrated from Indonesia. She lived in Northern California before moving to London to study art at Goldsmiths.

Contents

Legendary

He doesn't really talk about them. At least, he never tells me anything I want to know, their hang-ups or what kind of pretty they are. He tells only half a story about each of them, and he tells it three times. Verbatim, as if he has it written on the cuff of his sleeve. Normally he doesn't have two words to rub together, but when he does, something kind of flickers. These broken sparks and the three-times-telling make his exes seem mythical, crystalline.

When he tells me about Holly for the first time, we're at the movies sitting too close to the screen. We're watching the trailers and he's tracing shapes on the sensitive part of my wrist with his thumb. Every one of his exes has a *thing*— they've been molested or are a cellist or something. Holly shattered seventeen bones falling from a trapeze. She was wearing a cast and working in a library when he met her. Ten weeks later, when all the bones were knit, he finally saw her do her act. That's when he dumped her. He doesn't say, but I guess she must have looked too free and capable up there, swinging from the ropes. A girl like that could never honestly need you.

We're fighting and driving to the coast. His sister is marrying a guy he made out with at prep school, and we're late for the rehearsal dinner because I put the car keys in my coat and then packed it. After being quiet for twenty minutes he tells me about Holly again, a way of making up.

"Why do you like her so much better than the others?"

"What do you mean?"

"She's the only one with a name."

"That's crazy," he says.

He has one of those desks with a rolly top, and in that square, shallow drawer on the right is a manila envelope labeled TAX PAPERS with naked pictures of all of them. I open it only because I know he would never name an envelope "tax papers"; he would have separate ones for the different kinds of receipts and forms. The photos he's taken of me are still coiled inside his camera. At the time, he'd pretended it was a very spontaneous thing to do. I wonder why he thought he had to lie. Knowing what it was actually for would have made me want to do it more. I would have tried a lot harder.

I study their loose-limbed, puppyish bodies like flashcards. Is the margarine blonde with Satan eyes the one who got sick from the smell of blown-out candles? This one, freckles the color of fresh dirt sprayed across the bridge of her nose, she's the slow eater. Or she always left really long messages on his machine and used up the tape. Who could have raised show dogs and given him the clap? I hope it's the expensive one with the cheekbones, who's making a kiss-face.

Holly is the only one I know for definite; she's dangerous-looking with a muscly body, one arm a shade paler and thinner than the other. She's the worst kind of pretty: classically, mathematically gorgeous. I'm surprised to find that she's quite covered in long, white scars. Somehow I'd imagined the bones smashing inside her without any damage to the surface, but I guess there had to be. I picture the two of them standing on a bleached wooden pier, his arm wrapped around her, a choppy, salted wind ruffling her fawn-colored hair. He reaches under her sweater and traces his blunt fingers along those shiny ridges, the skin there impossibly silky. She is herself, unmistakably.

I teach myself to smile in a more teeth-baring way, showing off the little space between the two in front. I buy sunglasses, sign up for a night class in life drawing, and start to wear black. I laugh with my head flung back, saying ha-ha-ha instead of making suction sounds.

"Why have you started dressing like a Mafia widow?"

"I don't know what you're talking about."

I pencil in the mole beneath my left eye and sign up for two more classes: karate and Italian.

I wear my own clothes to work, but with a vest on top that has the Superman logo on it. It's meant to mean SuperCourier.

"This is probably too many classes now," he says when I deliver my karate uniform to the house. "Why didn't you just have them mail it?"

"It's cheaper this way. I used the employee discount."

He makes a face at my motorcycle.

"Can you get my sandwich from the fridge?" I say.

He sighs and goes inside. I did have the uniform mailed to me, but then I took it into work and logged it as a delivery. It's the best way of announcing things. He comes back out and gives me the sandwich.

"This is very sticky," he says. "What is it?"

"Bread and honey." I sit on my bike and eat while he paces around me.

"How's the art class, any good?"

"It's okay. I sit next to an old lady who draws only butt cheeks, week after week."

"What if the model is facing her?"

"She still draws their butt cheeks."

He stops pacing. It's very grown-up, the way he's wearing socks and shoes even though it's Saturday morning and he's just at home. "I don't get it," he says. "I mean, if you're going to sacrifice three evenings a week, you might as well take a real course, get a degree."

"I have a degree," I remind him.

He nods primly at the giant *S* on my chest. I look around for my clipboard.

"I didn't even know you wanted to be an artist," he says, exasperated. "How are you planning to manage all these classes?"

"I'll be fine," I tell him. "Sign here, please."

He does something with stocks and bonds, and gets a haircut every three weeks. He drinks bourbon from a glass instead of from the bottle. He wears the kind of shoes that need to be polished. Not a practicing Catholic, just chronic. Sleeps fetal. He's not my type but he has large, dry hands and a complicated nose with a deep dent near the top. I always think you can tell what someone is like in bed from the shape of his nose. And a knobbly Adam's apple, the white-knuckle kind you can see rise and fall.

He ties me to the brass bars of his sleigh bed. The guys I'm usually with barely have a box spring under the mattress. They own two appliances—a coffee machine and a bong—and a jumble of chairs. Furniture is something that's just supposed to happen to you. He on the other hand goes *antiquing*. I'm doing things I've never done before, such as picking up dry cleaning.

It's short but thick, and when he pushes it up inside he doesn't use his hands at all. He doesn't look me in the eyes, only at my mouth. He takes me to his druggy work parties and steers me around from room to room by the base of my neck. When he laughs his happiness builds just like a normal person's, but at the top his eyes go blank, as if there's nothing there.

I take the subway to night school. Lately it's always raining so I can't take the bike. Downtown, I switch from the southbound to the eastbound line. I run across the concourse, reaching the platform just as the train comes sliding in. The doors open to reveal a tangle of bodies, and I clock her immediately, that bone structure, the lean look in her eyes. As she brushes past me, everything snaps into place. I turn and follow her down the platform, watching her calf muscles flex.

"Holly?" I say, and touch her elbow.

She freezes for a second before turning around, like someone expecting to be caught. "Oh, I'm not her," she says. Then she looks right at me and narrows her eyes. "But you know, everyone always thinks I'm the person they're looking for."

We stand there, blinking at each other. She blows a tendril of hair out of her face and walks away. The train I should be on goes shooting past. I wonder if it's true that I'm looking for Holly. I must be, the way I just ran after this girl without even thinking. What if she had turned out to be Holly, what would I have said? There are things I want to ask her, but I don't know what they are. Yet maybe if I really were talking to Holly, I'd know.

The rain makes night school smell like what it really is, a high school at night. It's a teenage movie where everyone is at least thirty, lumbering down the halls and hunching around too-small desks. In Basic Italian I sit next to the woman who would play the best friend in the movie. She's technically prettier than me, the heroine, but not sexy enough. There's a coffee station set up at the back of the classroom, as if we're in AA.

When I get home, I go to his drawer and look at the pictures of Holly. They must have been taken in a hotel bed because there are light switches on the headboard. Her nose is slightly burnt, her scars and tan lines glowing. I pretend to slide his cigar fingers along their crests again. Her body is warm and crisp, pumped full of sun. We've never been on vacation. I practice her stubborn, innocent demeanor in the bathroom mirror; and later, when he's moving over me, I think of the constellation of beauty marks peppering her stomach and the underside of one breast.

During the break between gesture and long pose, everyone huddles outside in the rain to smoke except for me. The life models usually tie on their slippery kimono robes and nip out for one, too, but this girl perches naked at one of the desks and starts pawing through her bag. She wears two or three silver rings jammed onto nearly every finger and presses her lips tightly together, which somehow makes her seem fully dressed.

I watch her examining her skin in a tiny mirror. I didn't go to boarding school, and in college I roomed by myself, off campus—I don't know what women are really like or how they live. I almost had a sister, but she died before I was born. She was ten months old and had something wrong with her lungs. I found out about her only two summers ago, when I was still with one of the box-spring guys and his apartment was being fumigated. I didn't want to crash at his mangy friend's place, so I flew out to see my parents. They told me on the last night over lemon tagliatelle.

My father did the talking while my mother twisted a dishtowel and looked out the window and the tagliatelle shriveled.

"You could have told me earlier," I said. "What was she like?"

"I don't know. She was a baby," my father said. "She was always sick, so it was hard to see her personality. But she was cute."

"Very cute," my mother said. "Friendly."

"Oh, I see," I said. They're hopeless at describing people in a useful way. "So—what was her name?"

My father made a helpless gesture and turned to my mother, who shook her head.

"You've got to be kidding," I said.

"Now, don't be angry," my father said, as I stood up and pushed in my chair. "You have your own middle name."

I went into my teenage bedroom, where they keep their computer and all their vitamins, turned off the light, and stood in the middle of the room. I thought of the way my parents sometimes looked at me, glancing at a spot above my head and a little to the side. I crawled under the covers.

In the morning my clothes were all wrinkly. I went to the den and found my baby album in the games cupboard. I lay on my bed and looked at the pictures, getting a creepy feeling whenever I saw the crib or the stroller. My father drove me to the airport. He took my bags out of the trunk and put them on a cart.

"How could you?" I finally said as we went through the automatic doors. "Don't you know what that means?"

"It was a terrible time and we weren't thinking straight," he said.

The life model twists up a stick of bandage-colored concealer and applies it with stabbing motions, using her ring finger to blend the marks. Now and then she licks her fingertip. I can't stop watching her. I wish there were a channel on TV where all they'd show is women putting on makeup. There wouldn't be any sponsors to donate special equipment; everyone would use their own stubby pencils and smushed lipsticks, and rub them in with spitty, grubby fingers.

I'm sitting at his desk, slowly getting lit on the fifth of bourbon he keeps in a drawer. Holly fills my head like an annoying pop song. They must have met in this city. He's lived here for fifteen years. And she has to be nearby, somewhere. No one ever leaves.

His address book is by the phone. She's on the S page, with eight or nine phone numbers scrawled beneath her name in alternating colors of ink, all crossed out except for one. It rings a few times and the message clicks on.

"Hey, it's Holly. You know the drill." Her voice is soft and rough, a scraped knee. There's a sharp intake of breath, then the sound of the tone. I hang up the receiver.

In karate somebody hits me on the nose and it hurts so much I think it's broken. It happens during the jumping jacks; we aren't even sparring yet. My teacher is this ex-military hard-ass who won't let me sit out the rest of the class, even though my right eye swells completely shut and little droplets of blood and mucus keep appearing on the mats. On the subway, people wince and look away. I go to bed with scabs and snot crusted all over my face because it's too tender to wash.

In the morning the blinds are all lit up. He is inside me. "Hi," I say, and start to move. He holds me by one hip.

"Pretend you're still asleep," he says. "Okay? Try not to move."

Later he showers and goes to work. I lie awake for an hour, then sleep all day in short, dreamless bursts. Everyone grows older except for me. Briars creep across the city streets, enveloping the buildings.

Holly's address costs eleven dollars on a website where they look it up from when she last voted. I bike across town in the middle of the night to stand on her tree-lined street. She lives in a lumpen, gray building tacked to a row of brightly sparkling ones, like a bad tooth. I squint up at the windows on the third floor, their swampy television light and the plants on the sills. I shuffle to the building's entrance, and run my index finger over the cool buttons of the intercom. H SUNDEAN, it says, in slinky cursive on a strip of yellowing card stock. I peer through the glass section of the door at the metal mailboxes lining the narrow hall.

The following day, between deliveries, I duck into the bookstore on Twelfth Street. I rummage around in the basement until I find a paperback that's worn soft, the pages sprinkled with mould. Scribbled notes stuff the margins, spilling onto the typeface. On the first page in sloping fountain pen it says MR. CARL SPRING, and a date twenty years ago. During my lunch break I wrap it in brown paper and process it properly.

It's two-thirty in the afternoon when she opens the door, and her apartment is completely dark.

"Oh," she says, tugging the hood of a red sweatshirt over her messy, surfer-boy hair. She's coltish in her cut-offs and bare feet, small and tired and pretty. Her face is shaped like a heart.

"Are you expecting a package?" I say.

She takes it, smiling to herself in an entitled way. When I pass her the clipboard, her fingernail scrapes my skin.

"Sorry, I'm all—" She makes a vague gesture with her hands.

I look at her tiny, bare nails and picture them making deep crescents in his back. I smile at her and give her the pen.

She pulls a face. "That cigarette just about wrecked me. God, I feel awful."

"Hey," I say. "Listen. Would it be okay to use your bathroom?"

"Oh. Sure." She steps back and waves me through, and I notice she has a tattoo on the inner part of her wrist. I catch only a glimpse.

The apartment is warm and airless, overly furnished but

sort of empty, too. Nothing is out, not a photograph or a pair of scissors.

The bathroom is full of ferns, and there are seashells printed on the shower curtain. I lock the door and touch the bristles of her electric toothbrush. They're slightly damp. I inspect her toothpaste, her mint waxed floss and facial regimen. Apparently she has sensitive teeth and skin. In the mirror, I appear blank and marshmallowy, the way you do after too many magazines. Her medicine cabinet contains a blister pack of birth control pills and a sand-encrusted bottle of sunblock.

By the side of the tub is a wooden, cushion-back hairbrush with her soft, streaky hairs caught in it. Wound around its handle is some kind of child's ponytail holder with red plastic horses. I unwind it carefully and push it onto my wrist, rolling it under my sleeve and up to my elbow. When I come out of the bathroom, she has unwrapped the book and is leafing through it. She's like a little kid, kind of stroking the pages as she looks at them.

"Nice. Who's it from?" I say in a friendly way.

"I don't know. But look, it's all— Why would someone send me such a used book?"

"Maybe you sent them one," I offer helpfully.

"Huh," she says, annoyed. "Well, thanks."

"Okay," I say. "Thanks."

I find my clipboard and let myself out. As I kick up the stand on my bike, I realize I've completely wasted a turn. You can only meet a person one more time before the whole thing starts to look weird.

He's asleep. I cross the dark bedroom and lie on his legs.

"What," he says. He always wakes up instantly.

"Tell me about her for the third time," I say.

"Who?"

"But not about the library and everything—I've heard all that."

"Oh my God, you're obsessed."

"I know."

He laughs.

"Tell me," I say.

"Um. Actually, I bumped into her a few months ago. She still lives around here."

"Oh? How was she?"

"She looked amazing," he says.

"Okay," I say. "Great. And what happened, did you go for coffee or something?"

"Nah."

"Is she still a trapeze artist?"

"She gave it up because of a knee injury. Knees never heal all the way."

"Oh," I say, disappointed. From now on I'll always picture her in her apartment, smoking a cigarette. "What does she do instead?"

"Just anything, it looks like. When I bumped into her, she was spraying Christmas shoppers with perfume."

"But you and me, we'd go for coffee, right?"

"Yep, and cake, and broken-up sex," he says.

I glance up at him. "Seriously, though."

"Seriously?" he says. "Well, seriously, I'll have to now, won't I?"

The end of her street turns onto a bigger street where people are always walking up and down, so I wait for her here on the corner. It's a hot, bright evening with that vacuum-packed feeling before a storm, and I hope I won't have to bike home in the rain. I'll be glad when I give all this up. I'm here from just after five until six or seven most days. I see almost everyone in her building come home except for her.

I watch the women clipping past me in their heels. It's mesmeric, the way their asses tick from side to side like a watch on a chain, their polished limbs and blown-out haircuts glossy as sucked candy. The prettier they are, the faster they move. They brandish their carefully packaged bodies as weapons, as medals, as currency. I wonder what they'll do when they get back to their apartments. Probably they'll make salads and wear those camisole and boy-short sets that you see in the store and think, *Who even wears those?*

Later Holly emerges from her building dressed all in white. She walks a goddess walk like she's on wheels. I follow her two blocks to the Korean market and wander around, dropping random sachets and jars into my basket and looking at her through the shelves. Once, I go right up and stand with my back to her, pretending to read the labels of cans. We're so close I can smell her piña colada shampoo. I bump her with my shoulder, as if by accident. "Sorry," she says, moving down the aisle. I watch secretly from the deli section as she pays, the tattoo on her wrist flashing when she unzips her coin purse. It's something on fire with a tangle of thorns around it. Then she leaves, and I have to put back my groceries.

In one of the photographs she has her arms stretched above her head and you can see it clearly. I sketch it on the back of an envelope, then draw it on my wrist with a black Sharpie. I buy cigarettes and smoke one after lunch. It makes me dizzy. I dial her number again.

He wants me to strangle him while we're doing it.

"Just don't kill me," he says. "I should turn white but not purple."

We start with me on top, him lying with the belt loose around his neck. It takes a long time because I'm nervous and can't get off. When he's almost there, I slide the buckle up to his ear and pull and don't let go. I do it just the way he said.

Afterward I say, "Can't we ever make it straight?"

His eyes fog up like breathed-on glass. Behind them, my dollar is dropping.

At eleven o'clock in the morning on my day off, Holly strolls out of her building, tightly wrapped in a long coat and carrying a sort of case, like a hatbox. I tail her at a distance along the main street and down into the subway. When the train comes, I close in, climbing onto the same car. I stay by the doors, and she sits with her case on her lap. She's wearing so much makeup that her face looks like a drawing of a face. The flesh on her cheeks judders as we hurtle along.

She stands at the station exit, scanning the crowds, and I think she might be meeting someone. I interest myself in a blown-up advertisement, peeking around from time to time. A busker plays classical guitar, and a man on stilts hovers above our heads.

Holly plunks down her case in the middle of the sidewalk,

pops the latches, and removes a piggy bank, which she sets on the ground. Then she peels off her coat to reveal a shiny green leotard and pink trapeze shoes. She shuts the box, covers it with her coat, and stands on top of it, posing like a music-box dancer but letting her head hang. She stays frozen like that. People stroll by and some of them look at her, then at me watching her.

Finally a couple drops some change into the piggybank, but they don't hang around—they just keep walking. Holly does her act anyway. The premise seems to be that she's a kind of clockwork automaton locked in a display case. It's a combination of my two least favorite things: miming the existence of a glass box and robot dancing. But with the guitar music and the lattice of scars, it's sort of heartbreaking, as if she's tried and failed to escape before. Her movements are practiced and cynical, almost sarcastic. She spanks herself and swivels her hips, popping her joints to make it look like the gears are sticking. The whole time her expression is deadpan; her eyes open and close like a real doll's when you tip it.

As the money runs out, she gradually winds to a stop. By now a small crowd has gathered, and someone slips more coins into the slot. There's something so barefaced about the whole enterprise that I have to admire it. Other people—tourists—watch her with bemused smirks, their eyebrows slightly raised as if to say, *Is that it?* I feel like telling them who she is and what she's capable of. Someone snaps a picture. Holly blinks but forgets to mechanize it, unprepared for the flash. People walk away, bored. They make me so mad.

We've broken up but I haven't moved out, and I'm cutting his hair. He keeps shifting, trying to read the newspapers spread beneath his chair. His real hairdresser is away having a nervous breakdown.

"Will you please keep your head still?"

"Don't make it too short, or too even. I swear, last time she came back she could tell I'd had it cut by someone else. She made me look god-awful for two months."

"And you kept going?"

"She understands my hair."

"You should see a real barber—I don't even know what I'm doing."

All the lights are on and it's dark outside. We're reflected clearly in the kitchen window. He should give me the Motörhead T-shirt he's wearing. It looks so much better on me.

He's been dating an out-of-work actress who thinks I'm renting the spare room. I wonder why she isn't the one not-cutting his hair.

"How come you never bring her here?"

"Why do you think?"

"I'm looking at places," I tell him. "I saw two today."

"Uh-huh," he says. "Just, whenever. Anyway, she's not around."

"Where is she?"

"At a screenwriting course in Ann Arbor. Cheating on me. It's obvious."

"Are you sure?"

"I know her. She's lazy. She'll hook up with someone who lives ten minutes from wherever she has to be in the mornings. To her, an extra hour of sleep is worth having sex. I don't care. I'm getting too old to care whether people have sex without me."

"Oh," I say. This story isn't as good as the other ones. "What are you going to tell people about me?"

"Probably about how you kill bees, using your hands."

"Well," I say, "try to keep your head still."

I've taken the whole day off to move out, but by ten-fifteen in the morning I'm completely packed. It turns out nothing here was mine, apart from four kinds of loose leaf tea and the contents of the shower caddy. I cancel the cab I'd booked for this afternoon. I'll just take my things over on the subway and come back later for my bike.

I wander around the apartment, picking books and films off the shelves. I pull his Motörhead shirt out of the dryer. It's soft and warm, and there are still prickly bits of hair caught in the fabric. I take the tax papers envelope and the handheld electric beater for making iced cocoa, and lay them on top of the clothes in my suitcase.

I sit on the bed, scrolling through the numbers on my phone. I select the one labeled US. It takes a moment to connect. Holding the phone with my shoulder, I reach into the suitcase for the envelope. As the line beeps just out of sync with the phone ringing shrilly next to me, I slide out the photos and glance through them. At the bottom of the stack, beneath Holly's, I find the ones of me. The message clicks on. A recording of my voice echoes in the earpiece: "Hi, it's us. We're pretending not to be here—"

The sheets in the photographs match the sheets on the bed. The body looks good. The face isn't much. I smile. I'm one of them now, a blade in the guts of some future girl. I end the call and delete the number. I stuff the pictures back into the envelope and leave it in its drawer.

He calls me in my new place to ask if I can cut his hair again. I say fine, I'll come over later. I don't, and he never calls back.

I cross the wooded part of the park to the empty playground. I used to be able to see it from his bedroom window, the slide like a high-heeled shoe. The kids come here only at night to smoke joints on the merry-go-round. At the swing set, I hold the chains and do a running start, jump with both feet onto the sling seat just as it takes off. The chains squeak softly as I pump, standing tall on the rush forward, curling slightly on the roll back, wind zooming in my eyes. As I rock higher and higher, I can see why she liked it here. At the tip of the arc, my body is stretched parallel to the ground and weightless. I drift like that for a moment, staring down at the concrete and pretending it's a sea of upturned faces.

Date Night

'm watching an infomercial for spray-on hair for baldies and picking a scab on my knee when I hear the lift stop on our floor. I run to the dining room and pull the Yellow Pages out of the shoe cabinet. The doorbell rings.

"Don't answer it," my mother screams in Cantonese.

I like opening the door, but she only speaks Cantonese when she's totally stressed out so I guess I'd better not. The pages of the phonebook slide back and forth under my feet as I peep through the spyhole at Henry Shum, who has come all the way from Tai Koo Shing and is standing a bit too close, so he's just a giant nose. The TV audience is clapping. I hop down and patter to the kitchen, breathing in the sweet scent of chopped onions.

My mother's teetering on her highest heels and pouring macaroni cheese into a Pyrex dish, scraping the globs with a wooden spoon. Her face is colorful and plastic, and her earrings wink against her long hair that looks blacker and straighter than normal. She's been acting weird lately. She eats salad by itself as a meal, and when she's on the phone she laughs in this low voice, like *mm hm hmm*. She clacks over to the sink, her butt quivering beneath her dress that's dark pink and glossy, like lipstick. The doorbell rings again.

"Crap," she says, dunking the pan into the foamy water. Blobs of grey scum flick out and cling to her hair. She smoothes her skirt and yells, "Just a sec!"

"Why can't I meet him?" I ask, scratching a mosquito bite on the back of my leg with my big toe.

The oven rack makes silvery sounds as she slides the dish onto it. "Because," she says, banging the door shut, "he could still turn out to be an ass-hat." She presses the back of her hand to her forehead and looks at it.

"But you said he's great."

She gives herself a hard glance in the shiny black glass of the microwave.

"Everyone's great on the Internet, sweetie. That's what it's *for*." She sniffs her armpits.

"You have soap in your hair," I tell her. "Where's he taking you?"

"French food," she says, combing her hair with her fingers.

I follow her to the dining room. She clicks over to the shoe cupboard and starts moving things from her everyday purse to her clutch. I feel like she hasn't looked at me all week. After my father left, we lay in bed for days, staring into each other's eyes.

"Davy!" she calls.

Our new maid comes out of the hallway wearing yellow rubber gloves and clutching a blue sponge. She lives behind the kitchen, in the room that used to be the laundry room. She's small for an adult and stands very straight with her chin pushed down. She has a long ponytail, and big eyes peeking out from under her fringe.

"When you're finished, go to Movieland and rent some Japanese cartoons for Lily," my mom says, holding out a red hundred note and the membership card.

Davy takes them and slips them in the back pocket of her jeans. One finger of her glove gets trapped in her pocket and stretches very long before snapping back. She picks the phonebook up off the floor and puts it back in the cabinet.

My mom tucks her clutch purse under her arm. She checks the face of her watch, which she keeps turned to the inside of her wrist. "The macaroni will be ready at eight. Make a salad, and put sliced pears on it."

Davy nods. She points with her chin to the door. "He outside, ma'am?"

My mother grins at Davy like they're friends. "Will you take a look?" she says behind her hand. "I'm too nervous."

Davy smiles at me shyly and walks over to the door. I notice her toes are jumbly and spread. She goes up on tiptoe to peek through the spyhole, and turns to face my mom. "Good," she says. "Tall."

"Does he have three heads?" my mom whispers. "Is he a hundred years old?"

Davy giggles, padding back to the hallway, her ponytail swishing from side to side.

"Take a bath, and don't make trouble," my mother says in Cantonese, getting the keys from the big seashell and looping them over her finger. She opens the door narrowly, and squeezes through. "Sorry," I hear her say as she pulls it shut behind her.

The lock turns from outside. I get the phonebook from the cabinet and push it against the door, stepping up just in time to see the lift doors close. I go to the kitchen and pick up the handset of the entryphone to make the picture come up on the screen. It shows the sidewalk outside our building from above the lobby door. My mom comes walking out and Henry follows. She turns to say something to him, her eyes surprised and shimmery. I hang up the receiver and run to the living room.

On TV, the spokesmodel is interviewing a man who got married because of his fake spray hair. I stand on the sofa and slide the window open. We live on 5, but this is actually the fourth floor. They don't call it 4 because the Chinese word sounds almost exactly like the word for death. I see my mother and Henry crossing the road diagonally to a dark blue car parked in front of one of the furniture shops. A paper cup skips after them and the sidewalk trees crumple in the wind. My mother's bright dress flutters like a pink flame, and she glances up at the window with her long hair wrapped across her mouth. I can't see Henry's face, just his pencil-gray suit and the way he fits his hand to her back and pushes her towards his car. I picture them clinking glasses of wine over plates heaped with croissants and French fries.

I watch my mother sink into the blue car, pulling her long white legs inside, the evening sun flashing in her window as Henry swings the door shut and struts around to the other side, but I don't watch them drive away. I turn around to catch the end of the hair commercial. I'm dying to see how they actually spray it on.

I chew, pushing the Lazy Susan back and forth. The dark gray glass turns smoothly on the metal ring. One side is piled with snack foods in shiny packaging, pinched by Little Twin Stars clips. Davy sits sideways in my mother's chair, her arm resting on the table.

"Aren't you having dinner?" I ask her.

"I'm already eat." She has a cute way of talking, skipping words, and poking her tongue through her teeth when she

says the letters T and N and D. "Indonesian food." She pro-
nounces it *in the nation food*.

I swing my legs under the table. "Why? Don't you like macaroni cheese?"

She shakes her head very fast, as if she's scared.

"Indonesian food tastes better?" I try to say it the way she
did.

She nods, upwards.

"That's where you live?"

"Yah."

"What part?"

"Solo. I like because," she makes a fanning motion, "night
time not hot."

"It's cool at night?"

"Cool. Nice. I'm sleep good."

"I've been to Bali twice," I say.

She gets up and comes around to refill my glass. "I'm not
yet go to Bali," she says and goes and sits back down. I can see
a faint picture of the dining room in the window behind her.

"I first time Hong Kong," she says.

"Do you think you'll like living here?"

"I'm already very like it."

"Will you be homesick?"

She nods. My fork tinks the plate and the air-conditioner
makes a chugging sound.

"You like my country?" Davy asks.

"It's my favorite vacation place. I love the big swimming
pools, and the ice that looks like Christmas lights."

She opens her eyes very wide. "Apa, si?"

"The ice dessert, that's different colors?"

"Es campur. Nice for children. My daughter," she says, "she
very like es campur."

"You have a daughter? How old is she?"

She thinks for a moment. "Eight."

"I'm nine!"

"Yah. I'm already ask your mother. What her job?"

"She's an art director at a place called Ogilvy and Mather."

Davy's face turns serious. "I like art," she says quietly.

"What's your daughter's name?"

"Mega." She points to the window. "Cloud."

"That's pretty."

"I have photo," she says. "You want?"

I nod, bouncing my knees together under the table. She jumps up and goes off to get it. I eat the pears off the salad. Davy comes back carrying a carved wooden frame that must have taken up half her suitcase. She stands it on the table. The picture's stuck at the very back, so you have to peep in like you're looking into the window of a house.

A girl and a boy are holding hands and smiling from ear to ear. They have white teeth and white shirts and smart red neckties. The girl's hair is pulled back with a sparkly head-band. She has enormous eyes, and dimples drilled into her cheeks. The boy is taller, with bony knees and glued-down church hair.

I point. "Who's that?"

"Rafik. So naughty boy." She chuckles and starts clearing the table.

"Mega's so pretty," I say.

"She very good in sport and play guitar."

"I wish you'd brought her with you. I've always wanted a sister."

Davy tips her head to the side. She takes my dishes to the kitchen and returns with some mango halves on a plate. Instead of bringing me a teaspoon, she's cut criss-cross designs and turned the skins inside out to make porcupines. She sets them in front of me and disappears into the hall. I pick up a slab and start to slurp off the cubes. The juice runs down my chin. I hear the squeak of the faucet, and the tub filling. She comes back and stands next to me, looking at the photo.

"So does Mega live with her dad?"

"Mm-mm." She twirls the Lazy Susan until the box of Kleenex is in front of me.

"Who does she live with?"

Davy points to a woman's dress and some frizzy hair at the side of the photo. "Farah," she says. She goes and sits in my mother's chair and stares at the tablecloth.

I pull out a handful of tissues and blot my face. "Is Farah your sister?"

She looks up. "Rafik's mommy. She work here Hong Kong seven year. I'm—" she makes a motion like she's patting two invisible children who are getting taller.

"Oh, uh-huh."

"Now me." She nods.

"Your turn? For *seven years*? You won't see Mega in all that time?"

"My contract two year. I go Indonesia, come back, two year again."

"But then—why don't you take turns doing two years each? Wouldn't that be easier?"

"Not good to children, always change-change. Better long time."

"And when seven years is up, do you have to switch places again?"

"We stay home, open for business." She leans back, looking pleased.

"Is Farah your best friend?"

She smiles and shrugs. She looks at the front door as if she's expecting someone to come in.

"You must miss them. Do you have Skype?"

"Sky?"

"You know, talking on the computer?"

"Ah, Sky-pee. I'm not have this one."

"You can use ours. My mom won't care."

"Farah not have computer."

"Oh, right." Now I feel kind of bad for suggesting it. "I'm sorry."

"Okay," she says. "Air mail okay." She gets up and hurries off to check the bathwater. I put down the last mango skin. The sticky juice has reached my elbows. I dab them with the wadded Kleenex.

"Yah!" Davy calls.

I go down the hall to the bathroom, where she's stirring the water with her hand. I take off my clothes and get in. She squirts shower gel onto a body puff and sets it on the side of the tub, scoops up my clothes and goes away. I switch on the shower radio and listen to a show called *Non-stop Korean Love Ballad*. I practice holding my breath underwater. I finally manage to pick off my scab. The skin underneath is pink satin. As I'm soaping my arm with the puff, Davy comes back carrying my folded pajamas and underpants. Her hair's wet and combed, and she's changed into tracksuit bottoms and a T-shirt with ice-cream-colored elephants playing in a band.

"Do you want to watch cartoons with me later?" I ask her.

"I'm—" she sets the things on top of the dirty clothes basket and waves her arms around "—my suitcase."

"Oh, okay."

She leaves. I dip the puff in the bathwater and soap my other arm.

In the middle of the night, I stumble to my mother's room. There's no air-conditioner sound. I feel her bedspread and it's all smooth. I turn on the lamp. She's not here. I crawl across her bed to the window. The windows of the building opposite are dark. Normally you can look right into the bedrooms and living rooms and see people walking around and TVs flickering. I stand on the bed and lean against the glass, looking down into the street below. Greenish lights are on in the furniture shops, and the perfect living rooms and bedrooms look bright and empty. The world seems big and spooky, and like there's no one in it. I stand there for a while, waiting for a car to drive by or someone to come strolling along.

I wake up with the sun in my eyes. I turn away from the window and she's here, asleep in her pink dress. Her eyeballs are moving beneath the lids and she smells like smoke, and something bready. Normally she's naked, with headphones on and the cord wrapped around her neck, smelling of cucumber face cream. Her hand is up by her cheek and there's an ink stamp on the back of it. Her face looks strange and white in the sunshine. On her neck by her ear, the blueness of her pulse is a flashing light.

101

Northbound traffic's backed up all the way to San Rafael from Novato Narrows, where three lanes pinch into two. I've heard they're going to widen it next summer. The engine's idling rough, but I don't turn it off. I prop my chin on the steering wheel and squint into the boiling white sun, trying to picture your face.

I wasn't wearing my lenses that night in the pool. You were blurred at arm's length; your edges sharpening as you drew near. When I try to pull the image into focus, it breaks into fragments—the coarse grains of the pores on your cheeks, the feathery crosshatches on your lower lip—and even if I hold my breath and close my eyes, I can't make it whole again.

They got married at the end of the summer, before God and five hundred Korean people in a Gothic church on Wilshire Boulevard. The air-conditioning broke down and my sister hadn't slept; she was swaying as she muttered the words through her veil. For days we'd been trailing her and your brother in V formation. *Sibling along*, you called it, as we skirted banquet table archipelagos and glided across marbled atria and through jungly mezzanines. Once or twice we overtook them by mistake, and elderly relatives wished us a lifetime together, you and me. They thumped our backs and tried to press sharp-cornered envelopes into our palms.

In your kitten-gray tux, you were the best man, your silken hair wound into a ballerina knot. I was maid of honor in short satin gloves, with my crop fluffed, the cerise tea dress forcing good posture. Standing either side of the bride and groom in the sun-splashed chancel, we were taller, darker and leaner, like shadows. Our eyes locked as the minister declared them man and wife. When they kissed, we turned away.

The morning after the wedding, I woke up on a cot in my parents' hotel room. They'd taken off, trailing behind them a handful of empty pill casings and my mother's scent of leather and piano music. I switched on the TV and went back to sleep. In the afternoon I ate some airplane almonds. They left a burnt, wooden taste in my mouth. There was a knock and I opened the door. You had five o'clock shadow and faded eyes. You lay on the narrow bed with your shoes on, flicking channels while I packed my bag. By then, our siblings were in the Napa Valley, spitting wine into buckets and drifting in hot air balloons.

In the wavy heat of the parking lot, our clothes clung to our bodies. I saw hard twists of muscle in your back. We climbed into your brother's van. They'd forgotten their aviators on the dash. We slipped them on and faced each other, the silver lenses creating a mirror tunnel.

"We look better," you said, turning the key.

"Better how?"

"Older. Ice-colder."

You headed across Downtown, driving the same way as your brother, one hand at six o'clock, making corrections. I found my sister's lipstick in the change holder, the sunlight-through-eyelids red she's worn ever since she dropped out of flight school to study architecture. As I tried it on I heard you scrape the gears, and we ground to a halt. The lipstick smushed against my teeth. Car horns blared.

"Gah," you said, restarting the engine. "I've barely ever driven a stick before."

"I can see that." I tried to scratch and lick the lipstick off my teeth. We were moving, but people were still leaning on their horns.

"I've been bombing around all day, trying to get used to the gears," you said. "I'm supposed to drive it back up to their house, with the presents."

"What's it doing here? I thought they flew." I turned and looked in the back. "Will everything fit?"

"Yeah, easy. Most people gave money." You swung across traffic into a restaurant parking lot and backed us into a space. "I need someone to follow me in my car, so I'll have something to drive home in." You killed the engine.

"I'm flying back tomorrow."

"I can drop you off."

"College starts in two days."

You pulled up the handbrake. You unclipped your seatbelt and aimed your whole body at me.

"Fine," I said. "At least I know it's an automatic."

We went inside and ordered club sandwiches. We took off our sunglasses and smiled at each other.

When we'd almost finished loading the presents into the van, your mom came running out of the house and said we were supposed to open them first. My sister wanted us to take inventory in case the van got burgled.

"Really?" you said. "Does the car insurance cover it?"

"Of course not," your mom said. "But whatever happens, she has to send out thank you cards, right?"

I laughed at this. You sighed and started pulling things out.

We stacked the presents by the pool. The late afternoon sun formed hot stars on the water's skin. You unwrapped the gifts, detaching the cards and handing them to me. I covered one arm of the sun-lounger with little loops of Scotch tape.

"Weird, demented-looking statue," you said.

Exquisite sculpture, I jotted on the back of the envelope.

Most of the stuff didn't suit them. They're not the sort of people who would want to make their own candles or ice cream, and I couldn't picture them in matching sleep masks with unfunny sayings spelled in rhinestones. Stacked on top of the diving board were dozens of linen tablecloths brocaded with fish, flowers, or bats. Their dining table is glass-topped chromium steel. My sister cleans it with Windex four times a day.

"They've doubled up on so much stuff," I said. "Think they'll keep it all?"

"I don't see them keeping five rice cookers in a closet and working their way through, do you? It's too depressing."

"Right. They'll probably keep the nicest one of each thing, and give the rest away."

"They should give it to us," you said. "Why don't we elope and move into your sister's old apartment, with all of their unwanted stuff?"

"Good idea. We'll have all their exes come and live with us too."

"Yeah," you said. "Everything we have will be a slightly crappier version of what they have."

We laughed. We looked at our silhouettes lying on top of the water.

"Guys, I'm blocked in," your mom said. She was standing by the flipped-up garage door in a shiny blue Dodgers jacket. You tossed me your keys. I moved your car into the street and you moved your brother's van.

"Ciao," she said, zipping away in her Saab.

The sun was setting as we reversed the vehicles into the drive. We climbed out and slammed our doors. Our shadows reached across the tarmac.

"We should've taken the money Aunt Sylvia tried to give us," you said.

"I know. It could have been our nest egg."

I brought my bag into the house. You and your brother had been competitive swimmers and your mom's brown Seventies living room is packed with trophies and medals. I took out my contacts and put them in saline. Without them, everything looks like a photograph taken with trembling hands. I crouched behind the sofa, tugging on a one-piece with cutouts at the sides that I kept putting my legs through.

I slid open the patio door, my eyes still adjusting. You were a dark shape rising in the water. I watched you slash the surface with fast, tidy strokes, turning your head to alternate sides to snatch bites of air. I sliced in, the crisp scent of chlorine stinging my nose and mouth. I dove deep and flipped over. You floated above me, fanning your arms, the presents forming a quivering skyline as I swam up towards you.

Our heads popped through the surface.

"Welcome to our gene pool," you said, smoothing your hair.

I saw the shape of your skull, the way your bones wear the light. "It's a good pool," I said.

"Yeah. Legume-shaped."

Treading water, we gazed up at a large flat cloud of violet smog illuminated by city neon. The water was cool and soft, our breathing a little ragged. We turned and reached for one another, a fluid motion slowed by the water's resistance. As I pulled you towards me, fitting the pieces of your body to mine, I had the feeling I was putting something back together. You kissed me with the green apple taste of the pool on your tongue, kicking me as you pedaled to keep us afloat. I gripped your ribcage with my knees. Your skin was velveteen; your body thicker and denser than it appears. When I slid my hand into your shorts, you began to kick harder. You kneed me in the thigh and my teeth sank into your lip. Your blood tasted like the tip of a battery. You pushed me up against the ladder and folded me in half.

Later, bundled in towels, we polished off a plate of cold ribs. Your mom came home and pranced around the living room. Dodgers won. She started giving us the play-by-play and you sidled to the kitchen to throw away the oily cling wrap. While she re-enacted the ninth inning on the coffee table using candy from her purse, I glimpsed you outside, fishing my bathing suit out of the pool with a butterfly net. Later you handed me the soggy twist of fabric. I stuffed it in my bag. You made me a bed on the sofa and kissed me on the ear. You disappeared into the room where you'd grown up.

When I woke up I tasted pool water. My stomach hurt from the chemicals. The patio door was open, the sun's hard glitter strewn across the pool, and the presents were gone. I wondered if you'd left without me. One of the black machines beneath the TV had a time display, but the numbers were blinking so they couldn't be trusted. The moisture from my bathing suit had spread to the contents of my bag. I pulled on clammy, translucent clothes and walked into the kitchen, shivering. On the table were some breakfast things and a plate facedown. The tumble dryer hummed, zippers and buttons clicking against the metal drum. I padded back to the living room and you were there, folding the blankets. I pulled my top away from my skin to make it less see-through.

"Hi," you said, flicking your eyes up to my face. "Hey. Sleep okay?"

"What time is it?" I said.

"We should really—"

"Yeah." I zipped my bag and slung it over my shoulder.

We looked at each other.

"I hope it's not going to be like this," I said.

"No," you said. "It's not."

My flip-flops were by the patio door. I slid them on and shuffled to the car.

We left the city on Route 101, blending with Highway One in Oxnard, splitting just after the Gaviota Tunnel and merging again in Pismo Beach. In San Luis Obispo we broke away with the One. We made time, tarmac ticking by. I saw the contour of your jawbone reflected in your wing mirror. The sky was blue-jeans blue, clouds all smeared in one direction.

Gas station coffee tasted like the cup. You tipped yours out and it splashed across my windscreen, making a veil on the glass. I drifted in your wake, feeling the tug of your slipstream. I watched your cigarette hand in the wind, smoke threading your fingers. The blacktop sparkled, serpentine.

The sunlight looked like powder as you shoved me back onto the hood of the car. My shirt was off, and the metal was so hot the paint felt sticky. I unbuttoned your jeans. You took my wrists with one hand and held them above my head, rubbing a fist back and forth across my nipples.

"I don't have anything with me," you said, your hair closing around my face in a black sheet. I pressed my hands against the curve of your back. You moved my underwear to the side and pushed in.

I followed you up the part of Highway One that traces the raw Pacific coastline along a cliff edge. We'd hit it at exactly the wrong time of day, the sun in our eyes. My cell phone beeped. I picked up.

"Hey you," my sister said, sounding hyper and relaxed. "Where are you?"

"The One. I can't see a thing."

"At least you're on the inside of the curves. You'll hit some-one instead of falling in the sea."

"How's the place, is it nice?"

"Gorgeous. Tufa stone, and salvaged wood."

"Uh-huh."

"We got a massive upgrade. They gave our room away, and

then all they had left was a suite with a Jean-Marie Massaud bed. A Lipla. We have our own Zen garden."

"Stuff like that always happens to you."

She laughed. My sister laughs for longer than anyone I've ever met. No one else ever seems to mind. "We had lunch at the most incredible place. They served pear jellies and espresso sorbets between courses. Something about resetting the taste buds. Have you eaten?"

"We just—grabbed something."

"Okay, well. Love you," she said.

At a diner in Castroville, we sat by a window eating breakfast food and watching the sky turn pink and silver. You told me when you were a kid, you spent so much time in the water, all your dreams were set in swimming pools. Now you dream of the ocean. You surf every morning before class, and again at sunset. We left town on the 156, running onto the 101 beneath a bruising sky. Later I followed you into a sweetish mist. The city flashed blue and gold, and the lights on the bridge pulled tracers through the fog. Then hours of buzzing road, and green signs sizzling like ghosts.

The Redwoods glowed darkly in the aquarium light of the moon. I felt like I was driving across a dim, carpeted room. My cellphone buzzed and scuttled across the dash. I switched it to speaker.

"Should we be doing what we're doing?" you said.

I peered through the back window of the van up ahead, trying to see your silhouette. "I mean, I think we can do whatever we want."

"Well, sure. But you know, our families are connected. It's almost as if we'll be in business together for the rest of our lives. Maybe we're putting something at stake."

"I just don't see how it will ever affect them. It's not as if we'll get carried away and make this into a thing."

"Really?" you said.

"Well, because it's bound to fuck up. I mean, we're not them."

"Right," you said. "You okay to keep driving?"

"Fine. Coffee has me wired."

It was midnight when we pulled up in front of their building. We ferried the presents up in the elevator and piled them around the piano. Later as we sat on the L-shaped couch, laughing at the TV and passing a box of Cheerios back and forth, I thought I glimpsed a year or two of borrowing your sweaters and seeing you wear glasses at night. Your soft, shiny hair, clogging my sink.

As soon as you put it in, the phone began to ring. It kept ringing. The sun was bright and the lights were on.

"Their voicemail must be full," I said.

"Uh," you said.

"Should we pick up? It's probably them."

You just kept bumping me against the wall.

When you cut the engine, the music stopped. I could smell trees. It was night, but the sky above the dorm was blue.

"Thanks for the ride." I felt around for my bag on the floor.

"Can we do this? Think we should try?"

You almost touched my hair. I stared at the whitish knees of your jeans and then I climbed out and shut the door. For the first time that summer, the air was body temperature.

I walked up the steps. There were sputtering fluorescent lights and people carrying stuff around in laundry baskets. It was too late to get my things out of storage. I fetched my key from the RA and unlocked the door to my room. I went inside and sat on the sheetless bed.

By Columbus Day, I'd had two missed calls from you. A few days later, a pink plus sign appeared on a stick. I went to the store and bought another stick. Both sticks agreed. I phoned my sister and she picked up right away.

"Oh my God, sister telepathy," she said. "I was just about to call you. I'm pregnant!"

"Jesus," I said. "Wow."

"We're not telling anyone for three months, not even Mom and Dad, okay?"

"Sure, I understand. Hey, congratulations."

"Thanks. We think it happened on our honeymoon. Isn't that neat?"

"Aw. So neat. Uh, listen, can I call you back a little later?"

"We're going out, so maybe tomorrow?"

"Yeah. Great."

"Byeee," she said.

I put down the phone and covered my face.

I had a scan where they hid the screen. I swallowed a pill. I sat on a chair in a pale blue room, drinking from a paper cone. I unstuck my thighs from the pleather and went home. I came back a few days later and pushed four pills inside. I lay behind a curtain, the music in my headphones sounding sugary and angelic. I bled into a tray. Someone came in sometimes to empty it. I tried not to picture a small red heart or tiny ribs or muscles. In the evening as I waited for the bus, you phoned. I didn't pick up.

I started calling my sister almost every day. I drove up to see her. I felt the bump. She read me stroller specs and detailed descriptions of what the fetus looked like. She told me it had fingerprints and eyebrows. We spent hours on the phone, holding names in our mouths, rolling them against the name you share with your brother. I went into stores and bought things and sent them to her.

At Thanksgiving, she told me you'd been seeing someone. I gave her sharp bones and cellophane hair. Skin that burns. Over Christmas, your brother said you were in Costa Rica. I pictured you and her in jeweled waters, doing Eskimo rolls beneath the oncoming waves as you paddled your longboards out to the line-up.

Around Easter I received a letter from my sister. I slipped it in my bag and went to class. A few nights later I was sitting on my bed, writing a paper, when it fell out of the pages of my textbook. I opened it. It was a card with a photo of unlaced baby shoes on the front, an invitation to the shower. At the bottom, she'd scrawled in her boyish handwriting: IT'S A GIRL! (WE THINK).

Tucked into the card was a Xerox of her latest ultrasound. All of the earlier scans had appeared to depict distant galaxies, but here, you could see the baby folded up, a hand curled against its cheek. My mind started flashing all the pictures that would follow this one. I saw them riffle across the bed like a croupier's stack. I knew I was destined never to forget: I would always know how old, which grade, an approximate size. On the morning of the shower, I made my excuses. When the birth announcement came in June, I mailed a check.

I've stayed in the city all summer, punching a till and swimming at the Y. On bad days I'm still afraid. I think the baby's a ghost, a reproach or even a punishment for what I did, or didn't do. On better days, I wonder if she might be a window into a parallel universe. A mirror, in which fates are reversed. A card arrived last week: white, with a small white cross, an invitation to the baptism. That tiny wrench turned inside me just the same, but before too long the feeling went away.

I fill the tank at a gas station overlooking Arcata Bay. I buy a soda and drink it sitting in the car with the door open. The service begins in an hour. I'm scared of seeing you, scared I'll look into your eyes and you'll know. Or worse, you won't. They'll probably force me to hold her and breathe her scent. I think I'm lucky. Most people never know exactly what they've missed.

The water in the bay shines like ice. I pull the invite out of the glove box to check the address and a photograph flutters out. She has tufty, rockabilly hair and your triangular eyebrows. My defined cupid's bow. She reminds me of my sister and me in our baby pictures, but you can tell she's from a different generation. She appears more poised and person-like, more together than we were. She seems smart and modern somehow.

Julia K.

We met in the metal garden and smoked on top of the slide. It was usually dark, and in the dark her words emerged as a lit cortège, cutting the horizon.

"When I grow up," she said, "I want to be a disease."

Language, as she deployed it, was neither a line cast nor a bullet fired. It was a catholic mechanism: the sharp twist of a pilot biscuit into the waifish body of a christ. A word, placed on her tongue, became flesh. One night it was almost morning, I could almost see her, every sentence a necklace she was pulling out of her mouth, tangled in smoke.

"I want to be filthy with beauty," she said, "loaded on stink and swagger. I want to be heart on bicep, balls in throat, with my best friend's eyes in my pocket, and a flaming comet of hunger clutched in my fist like a pet rock."

She had a large, stretchy mouth and spoke like an X-ray, stripping every word to bone. "I want to be a jet-fuelled mass of chrome and steel, circling the planet with an infinite supply of packaged almonds, missing no one, my strong, clean body rippling in the heat that rises from the landing strip, my little feet, wheels that never fail to find it."

"I want doll skin," she said, "sticker eyes. I want to be a

black flash of lashes against a desiccated white lie, stamped with a smooch. I want bendable limbs, high-heeled feet and a plastic snatch.

"I want to cut teeth. To break bones in the street and use the pieces to draw pictures with my blood on the sides of buildings. I want to be the city melting behind the glass, and I want to be the glass, inlaid with wire mesh so when it breaks it hangs together still. And I want to be the breaks.

"But I know what I am," she said then, "I'm like you: the sweet spot, the rough patch, the missing rib.

"I'm the coyness, the wheedle, faked passion, icicle tears, small betrayals, the accommodating orifices, the warm welcome and the long way back. I'm the pout, the prettiness, and dreams of the real thing. I am hard knocks and lost loves. I'm just like a real person—in a movie. I'm how much it hurts and how much that's part of it."

She finished her cigarette. I leaned in to taste her mouth. It tasted bloody and torn apart. When I smeared her against the slide, she was a true thing bursting open in silver pieces against the pale fresh silent playground.

Later, I lit up and she stayed lying down. Each time I pulled on the cigarette, the cherry burned a short film of her face moving against itself, the way rain wriggles down glass. There was something horrific in it. I let my smoke rise, and then I fastened my belt and walked away.

It was spring when I saw Julia again. She lived above me, crying in the bath and moving furniture at night in high heels, but I only ever ran into her in the playground across the street from our mansion block. I was happy to see her. I liked her golden eyes and big waves of hair, her candlelit skin. There was something deluxe and unfathomable about her form. It seemed in continuous, almost imperceptible motion, like a body of water. She said she'd been to visit her father, she didn't say where. As she sparked up I noticed a raised pink button of scar tissue, the size of a pencil eraser, on the back of each hand. I wondered if she'd been away long enough for these to be new, and if not, why I hadn't noticed them before. It had rained and the world was black glitter. I listened to the suck and pop of her lips on the filter, the sizzle of burning paper, and her delicate, agonized sighs.

She invited me to supper. "To celebrate," she said.

"Is it your birthday?"

"My anniversary."

"Ah," I said, flashing on the way she'd arched her back and gripped the sides of the slide. "Happy anniversary."

"Thank you." She blew a smoke ring and poked it.

I was surprised. Julia exuded such an air of freedom and solitude that I'd assumed she was single, and possibly an orphan. We left the playground and crossed the road, splashing through the puddles.

I could smell hot, scented oils. The flat was dark and glossy, all leather and blood-colored wood, and she didn't try to make it brighter. When I looked around, I felt as if I'd died and someone else had moved into my apartment. There was no one waiting, and nothing on the dining table except a salmon-pink plasticky paper cloth, its sticky sheen reminiscent of scar tissue. I began to suspect that the person with whom she shared this anniversary was out of town, perhaps even out of her life, and I was to be their surrogate. I wondered how far I'd be expected to deputize the role. She poured me a glass of watery wine to drink while she made Bloody Marys. She mixed in Angostura bitters and celery salt, and scrambled a panful of eggs.

"I'm tomorrow's girl today," she said, dishing all the eggs onto a plate and sliding it across the table.

The eggs were runny and transparent in places, yet I couldn't be sure whether the black bits were pepper or charcoal.

"Aren't you going to have any?" I said.

"I don't eat eggs." She retreated to the kitchen and returned with a jar filled with rollmops suspended in cloudy liquid, and a box of saltines. A woman in a black chādor emerged from the master bedroom, pushing a metal walking frame. Only her long white hands and almost mouthless face were visible. Her eyes shone like olives. She looked like Julia might look if she became an owl.

"My mother," Julia said, unscrewing the jar, "she doesn't speak."

I said hello. The mother nodded demurely and wobbled towards the couch. She wore squeaky red pumps that ticked against the floorboards as she scraped the walker along. I realized this was the sound I'd been hearing at night. I decided it was her, sobbing in the tub. She switched on a true crime show and cranked up the volume.

"You mean she doesn't speak English?" I shouted over the blare.

"She's taken a vow of silence," Julia said, plopping a rollmop on my plate. "She had a vision when she was pregnant with me. My father says she was just dehydrated, but I believe it was something."

"You've never heard her speak?"

"She prays out loud."

I was starting to get a poppers headache from the scent

of the oils. The TV blasted a detailed blood spatter analysis and the pickled herring was gelatinous and hairy. I prodded the eggs with my fork. I looked at the wide, smooth bones of Julia's face, her lips that always looked bitten, unable to grasp how such a beautiful woman could be responsible for this revolting food. I glanced at her mother, who was sitting there like a monolith. I wondered whether the cloak was a cultural or a personal accoutrement. I couldn't place Julia's ethnicity. She could seem Brazilian, Jewish, Jamaican or Irish, as her mood shifted. She had been rather quiet since we entered the flat.

"What do you do?" I asked her.

"I'm a laser technician."

I pictured beams of blue and violet light shooting from her fingertips. "What does that mean exactly?"

"I remove tattoos, mostly. Sometimes freckles, hair, and port-wine stains."

This didn't sound like it would pay well, and I wondered how she could afford to live in our building. I forced myself to take a bite of the eggs. They were lukewarm and slimy, and I tasted the grit of eggshell. I put down my fork, trying not to gag. Julia took my plate to the kitchen and reappeared with a paring knife and a bowl of figs. Finally, something she couldn't destroy. I sliced one open and broke it apart. I'd never noticed before how fig flesh resembles putrid, maggoty meat. I dropped it on the table and pulled out my cigarettes.

"We have to go outside," Julia whispered. "She doesn't know I smoke."

I excused myself to go to the bathroom. I could hear a slapping sound behind the door. When I pushed it open, I saw a huge black fish splashing in the bath. Something about its rubberiness, on top of everything else, made me want to be sick.

I flipped up the lid of the toilet, but I didn't want the fish to watch me throwing up, so I went into the hall and leaned my head against the wall. My stomach turned every time I heard the fish flop. I noticed that the door to the smaller bedroom was ajar. I could hear Julia banging around in the kitchen, so I nudged the door and went in.

There was a desk, a chair, crammed bookshelves, and books stacked knee-deep on the floor. A ballet barre ran along the bottom of the window and the desk was piled with sentences handwritten on strips of paper. Some were arranged on the desk like refrigerator poetry. I noted the absence of a bed. I knew the flat had only two bedrooms, but I resisted the notion that she slept next door with her mother. It just seemed too bizarre. I pictured her asleep on top of the books with snowy drifts of cut-out words forming a pillow and duvet.

In the playground Julia held out her fists, like she was sporting LOVE HATE tattoos. The smoke laced her fingers and I looked at her keloid scars.

"This was seven years ago," she said, as if she was showing me a photograph. "I was working as a pole dancer."

"No shit. What was your stage name?"

"Proust."

I laughed. "Any special reason?"

"I wanted to hear the announcer say it in his schmoozy voice when he introduced my act. Anyway. There was a patron who didn't come in very often, maybe once a month," she took a drag like a last breath, "always alone. He was tall and slender, with half-European, half-Asiatic features that were so chiseled it seemed almost grotesque. Bright amphetamine skin and pointy black shoes. Instead of tucking fivers into my G-string, he'd slip me a long white envelope containing a cashier's check for a few hundred quid. But first, he always reached up as if to shake my hand.

"When I offered my hand, he slid his palm past mine and circled my wrist with his fingers. I felt a lift, like a drug rush, and he let go. No one was allowed to touch us, but since I appeared to initiate the contact, and because it looked so out of place, I suppose, the bouncers never stopped him. This went on for months. The mixture of need, anticipation and gratitude established a bond. Sometimes when I was leaving the club or my building, I had the feeling I was being watched. One night the envelope was fatter and I thought he'd given me cash, but inside was a contract."

"A job contract?"

"I won't say how much he offered me, because that would be naming my price, but it was *a lot*. The contract had four clauses: I wasn't to eat or to wear underwear or socks for four hours beforehand, or to press charges afterwards, and I shouldn't be intoxicated. The final condition was a gag order lasting seven years. It expired today."

The pieces clicked into place. "This is the anniversary you meant?"

"It's been in the vault all this time."

"You mean you actually honored the agreement? Why?"

"It's just good form," she said, shrugging. "I always keep my promises."

"What did he want you to do?"

"He'd listed all the things he didn't want to do. Like he didn't want to fuck, photograph or film me, or cook and eat me, or piss or shit on me. I didn't have to drink his come or pass it to anyone else's mouth."

"Hmm."

"It went on like that." She lit a cigarette off the one she had going and blew smoke through her nostrils. "No enema was necessary. I wouldn't have to change my name or get a tattoo. I'd be acting my own age. I wouldn't have to smoke, or to masturbate. I wouldn't be tickled or scratched or bitten.

"There would be no candle wax, coffins, speculums or cattle prods involved. I wouldn't have to wear a diaper, a straitjacket or a labial clip. I'd be allowed to keep all of my hair. I wouldn't be acting like an animal, a waiter, an ashtray, a toilet, or any piece of furniture.

"There would be no abrasion. No dolls. I wouldn't be asphyxiated, inseminated, branded or breastfed. I wouldn't be fucked with feet or have to use a chamber pot, and he didn't want to do that thing where you squeeze your legs together to form a triangular saké vessel.

"No telephones, animals or electricity would be used. I wouldn't be mummified in cling film or otherwise, or have to do any chores. I wouldn't be force-fed or entered into an auction. Pages and pages of this shit.

"Even just by reading the contract, I was already playing the game. I could picture every fascination he'd described. It was as if we'd done all those things and I already belonged to him."

"Did you consider refusing?"

"I don't believe in turning things down. And I was young, a little unsure of my worth. I liked the idea of being paid that much to do something that, apparently, only I could do. Most of all, I wanted to know what a person might want so much. If I didn't do it, I'd never find out. I signed the contract, filled in my bank details and completed the health questionnaire, which included some unusual measurements. I mailed it to his PO box. About a week later, a long white envelope arrived without a postmark. It contained instructions for my pick-up. As the day drew near, I began to look forward to it in a peculiar sort of way.

"I went to the meeting place at three in the afternoon. It was a street address with no floor number so I thought it would be a house, but it turned out to be a garden next to a cemetery. I arrived just as the rain cleared. The flowers looked beaded and swollen, and the marble tombstones and stone statues glistened in the sunlight.

"A white van reversed through the gates. I went over and opened one of the back doors and climbed in. There was a metal bulb stuck to the floor that followed me like an eye. The windows were sealed, and when I closed the doors it was so dark I couldn't tell if my eyes were open or shut. As we started to move, I crouched on the floor and took off my clothes, as I'd been instructed. The glinting eye watched me.

"The sound of car horns and jackhammers faded. We drove in a straight line, without stopping, for what seemed like a few hours. The road surface changed and we took some wild turns. The van stopped, and the engine cut off. The floor shuddered when the front doors slammed. I waited for someone to come and let me out. I could hear sounds in the distance, water rushing and children squealing. The noise grew and faded, distorting as if going around a bend.

"I crawled across the floor, feeling for the doors. I found the handles, but they wouldn't turn. I started shouting and banging on the metal. When my hands were sore, I lay on my back and hammered the doors with my feet. I wondered if I was going to die there, while the camera watched. I curled into a ball on my side and cried. Next thing I knew, I caught a knock to the chin that made me bite my tongue so hard I saw sparks. I was bouncing in the back of the van and we were going very fast, off-road. We slowed down and crunched up a slope. Then we reversed and braked, but the motor kept running. I heard a clicking sound. The doors swung slowly open.

"It was night. Out in the cool, blue forest stood a statuesque woman with a shaved head, holding a rope. I climbed out and walked unsteadily towards her. She had bare feet and long toes and wore a long-sleeved chainmail leotard that glittered in the taillights. I thought she was the man's sister. The overt beauty that had appeared almost repulsive on him was wonderful on her. She took my hands and placed them together as if in prayer, and tied my wrists together. I thought I recognized the temperature of her touch. When I tried to summon a memory of my patron, all I could picture was a suit, a cipher—I realized it would have been easy to pass in the polarized atmosphere of the strip club.

"She led me by the rope through the trees. I tried to read the line of her body, but I couldn't tell if this was the same person or not. Waiting at the edge of the forest were four men with flashlights. They wore metal masks shaped like horses' heads, and one of them held a black box with a handle. The masks were very tall, so that the men's faces were in the horses' necks. I didn't know how they were able to see.

"We walked across the meadow and up a hill. The men wore toolbelts that clanked as they walked. It felt so creepy, marching across the countryside in this secret procession. When we reached the top, I saw a makeshift scaffold and, lying flat on the ground beside it, a life-sized wooden cross with cables snaking out. The men switched off their torches and the woman let go of the rope.

"They formed a circle around me, the men with their masks on, me with my wrists tied. There were no trees, and a three-quarters moon had come out. The woman said something that was a command without being a word, like an acrobat giving a cue, and I felt one of the men come up behind me and take something out of his belt. I wanted to turn around but I was afraid, so I shut my eyes. He started brushing my hair. He did this for quite a long time. The bristles were sharp and stiff.

"The woman untied my hands, and two men picked me up by the armpits and ankles and laid me out on the cross. There was a short bar extending between my legs and a platform for my feet. They fastened my arms to the crossbeam just above the elbow and at the wrist, with multi-stranded cable that threaded right through the wood, and fixed my knees and ankles to the standing beam. One man had a special machine that clamped and melted the cable—I could smell hot plastic and wire. Another went around trimming the ends with wirecutters.

"The way everything fit my body, and was so ultratech, made me feel almost safe. The woman knelt beside me, and the man with the tallest horse's head came over with the metal box. He unsnapped the latches and opened it and started passing things to her: a pair of latex gloves that she put on, and some make-up sponges, which she tucked into my arm restraints, making them tighter. She flicked my veins and swabbed them with a cotton ball soaked in chilly pink liquid. The man gave her two syringes, clear and cloudy. Holding one between her teeth, she uncapped the other and emptied it into my arm. Whatever it was, it burned going in. She dropped the used syringe into the black box and stuck a small round plaster over the puncture wound before injecting my other arm.

"When she removed the sponges from under the cable ties, one arm felt hot and the other felt cold, and then they both felt like air. The man took out a long thin nail and started to hammer it through my palm. I could see the blood streaking and feel the pounding of the mallet vibrating in my teeth and eye sockets, but I was numb from the neck down. They didn't put nails in my feet. It would have caused too much damage."

She opened her hand and pointed to the satiny disc. "See how it's not perfectly centered? They went between the bones. This spot is symbolic anyway. You'd have been nailed through the wrists. So then the woman was kneeling beside me again. She had a tiny pot that looked like lip balm, and she twisted it open and dipped her index finger into it. Her movements had a loopy, layered quality, and I realized my eyes were strobing. When I tried to look directly at anything, my focal point kept oscillating either side of it. The stars looked like needles.

"Her outstretched finger was covered in gold paint and seemed unnaturally luminous. I had an impulse to touch it, but my hands were nailed down. The brightness seemed important, and sexual. I began to feel turned on, not in the human way, but as if I was a plant, photosynthesizing. When she daubed the paint on my forehead, my skin seemed to feather beneath her touch, like an eye opening. She put her finger in her mouth and sucked off the paint. The gesture struck me as unbearably raw. It just about doubled me over. I've never experienced anything like it—I felt like I was going to burst. The feeling subsided, and I felt pure and spun, like after a crying jag. I got lost in her face for a while. When she opened her mouth, I saw a galaxy inside it.

"The men threw the cables over the scaffold. They winched me up and forward, and I heard hammering. Within seconds, I began to feel the strain. If I let myself hang from my arms, my chest felt tight and I had trouble breathing. I had to push against the platform with my feet and keep my whole body engaged. You need a super-strong core. I guess that's why she didn't just pick some girl off the street."

She lit two cigarettes and handed one to me. "That's when I started to see shit."

"What kind of things?"

"Winged embryos flying through the sky. Gods fucking each other with snakes coming out of their eyes. I saw a tribe of glass people holding weapons and tools made of skin. They had shiny transparent bones and organs nested inside their bodies, and real blood in the mesh of their veins.

"I saw hundreds of people walking through darkness and light. Young and old, through sun and snow. Some walked on their knees.

"I saw a boy with shells covering his body, swimming along the ocean floor. Sometimes a single pearl of air escaped from his lips. When he came to an underwater volcano, he hovered beside it until an octopus rose from its mouth. The boy's legs scissored and he shot towards the octopus and bit it between the eyes.

"I saw a tall, bearded man in a red cloak banging a drum and dancing on giant stone steps. The cloak had a hood that looked like a girl's face with blond hair and a bloody heart attached.

"I saw four children kneeling on a bed and peeping through a window into a moonlit garden, where a man and a woman stood facing one another. While the man wore simple clothes, the woman was sheathed in a gold silk dress with a high neck, her wrists and ankles dripping jewels. She got on her hands and knees in front of him and pressed her forehead to the ground.

"I saw a desert, so vast it hugged the planet's curvature. The sky was egg-yolk yellow, and the sun and sand were white tinged with violet. Thousands of statues stood in perfect rows. There was a ripple as they tipped their faces towards the sun. They were still again, so still I wondered if I'd imagined the movement, if they'd been positioned that way to begin. At some unspoken cue, they began to move in perfect unison. It was a slow dance, a sequence of poses. The figures moved in impossible ways. No two steps were exactly alike, it was a progression or a story. When the dance was complete they stood still, their faces upturned. There was a crackling sound and the sun's edge blackened as if burnt by flame. As the shadow slid across the sun, the figures bowed. The darker the sky grew, the deeper they bowed. The bluish corona appeared. Perfect, it quivered and was gone.

"It was dark. I was thirsty. When I sat up, I saw the metal eye and knew I was in the van. It wasn't moving. Crawling across the floor, I could feel that my hands were bandaged. I clambered out and shut the doors. I looked around. I was on a quiet residential street. It was dawn.

"As the van pulled away, I felt like I was re-entering Earth's orbit after being away a hundred years. I couldn't remember anything about myself. I wasn't even sure if the clothes I was wearing belonged to me. It took me a while to recognize where I was standing, at the end of my road. I went home and took off the bandages. My wounds had been neatly sewn up. The next day, the money landed in my account.

"For months, I barely spoke to anyone. I just felt very spaced all the time. All I wanted to do was stay in my room, listening to music. Then one morning I woke up and went outside. It was autumn and the sunlight was knives, cutting through my body. When people passed me on the street, I could look into their eyes and see what color the sky was at the moment of their birth. What color it would be when they died. I could move through their whole lives, even things they hadn't done yet, as easily as walking through the rooms of a house. It wasn't like flashing images—more like knowing where your tongue is in your mouth so you don't bite it.

"To me, other people used to be a show that was on sometimes, like fish at the aquarium, and now, I could feel everyone around the world at once, in painfully exquisite detail. When this faded after a few weeks, I was relieved. But I started to wonder if what had happened was something I needed. I went back to the club to look for her, hoping to find out what else she wanted to do."

"Did you see her?"

"I did, eventually. Before I could approach her, she walked up to the stage, holding an envelope. I saw her do the handshake on this other girl. Then she took a step back, slipped the envelope back into her pocket, and left. The club burned down a few weeks later."

It began to pour. We were instantly drenched, and Julia's hair frizzed into a ball. We laughed as we slid down the slide and ran across the street. We stepped into the elevator, wet and shivering, and I pushed her up against the doors as we began to rise.

Kissing Julia was like kissing language. Her tongue was a flame, licking phoneme and diphthong. She swallowed me like a sword and her eyes were doves, her mouth a lake of fire. Her cunt a cup of tears. Her body a city: I carved a key out of soap, found the trapdoors and learned the secret knocks. I drew a map and held it inside me, the dark, oily streets running through me like veins. I chalked hopscotch grids on pavements and wrote on walls. I watched leaves fall and animals die. The sun turned black and when she pressed her thumbs against my windpipe, I heard galloping horses and the hard bass of gunfire. We came like dragons, heaven and earth getting closer. Her eyes blazed red and gold, and in them, kingdoms burned.

In the morning she was gone and there was ash on my pillow.

I stopped going to the playground. I started smoking in the flat, out the kitchen window. I wasn't sure about the choking, and I didn't like the way everything seemed darker and brighter around her. One night as I was coming back from work, I looked up and saw her watching from her dining room window. I realized I hadn't heard any scuffling from upstairs in a while. The lamp shone through her hair as she smiled. I waved and she disappeared. I thought she might be coming downstairs, so I hung around by the letterboxes until some other people came in. The following night I went upstairs and rang her doorbell. A little girl in a ballerina costume answered. She said she'd been living there since before the Easter holidays, but she also told me her parents were unicorns.

Last week, I was in another city. Julia was there, in a black bar on a black street, holding a dark drink.

"You again," she said and took a sip.

I offered her a cigarette. She said she'd quit.

DD-MM-YY

kick off my shoes and roll my suitcase down the hall to my room. When I turn on the light, I see a bump under the bedclothes, and pink and yellow hair piled on my pillow. That's Coney. She grew up next door. Her family moved away, but she still has a key to our house. Her skirt and bracelets are on the floor. I switch off the light and go and knock on Marc's door. I open it.

The desk lamp's on, and his hand luggage is on the bed. Shit, now I owe him fifty dollars. Our colleges break up at the same time but he always beats me back. He must skip out early. He can't stand to lose a wager. I go out to the deck to look for him. There's a towel spread across one of the loungers, and his Camels and lighter are on the picnic table. The pack's almost full. I ease one out and spark it up. I blow out the smoke. The swimming pool glows in the dark. My parents are away. I've forgotten where they went.

Marc and I always tell people we're twins, but we're actually triplets. The third son was stillborn and in biology class I learned that we probably killed him. I believe it. We're still kind of like that. I phone Marc, and he picks up right away. I can hear music and laughter and splashing.

"Ha ha, you lose," he says. "Suck a bag of cocktips, you fucksqueek."

"Dicklick," I say, moving the towel so I can sit.

"Cumface."

"Soapy titjack."

"Diarrhea weenieclown."

"Ball juggler."

"That isn't a thing, you anal dildo," he says. "We're at Galen's. Come, and bring my smokes. You fucking scrote, you're smoking one right now."

"I'm not. I've quit," I say, exhaling away from the phone. "You didn't tell me Coney was coming."

"Huh. So she made it back."

"Was she out with you?"

"She got too mash-up. I had to put her in a cab."

"Fuck, man. She wasn't moving. What if she's ODing again?"

"Why do you think I told her to lie in *your* bed?" he says.

"You're an asshole. Worse. You're a jackhole."

He laughs. "Come, dummy. Let's have fun."

I can hear a girl talking to him. "Babe," he says, "can't you see that Daddy's on the phone?"

I roll my eyes. I share DNA with this person. "I'm tired," I say.

"Stop being such a period."

"Maybe I'll come down later." I put out my cigarette and go back inside.

"You're the jackhole, jackhole," he says and hangs up.

My brother used to be some kind of expert who could tell you all of the best things. He knew when to pick off a scab so the skin underneath would be gray and sticky and tight. He could turn Coke into beer and pull wings off butterflies. Now he doesn't know shit. I make a peanut butter sandwich and eat it over the sink. I go to my parents' bathroom and take some of my mother's Seconal, cupping my hand beneath the faucet. I lie on their bed, waiting for the pills to land.

Coney's parents worked a lot, so she was always over here playing Xbox. She was class valedictorian and better than your average girl, but otherwise normal, waiting for the school bus in her mittens, and swimming in our pool until her hair turned green. The summer we were fifteen, her face and body appeared. My brother started a band with her, like he always does. Coney streaked her hair pink and sang lead vocals, and Marc programmed the drums, played synth and sang back-up. The weird thing was, they were tight. They sounded like a real, grown-up band. Their songs were all about love and machines. They never wrote anything down.

We passed our driving tests around the time DD-MM-YY started booking gigs. I was their roadie. One night, coming back from a show, Marc and Coney were fighting about a girl. Marc was driving, and Coney and I were in the backseat with the midi keyboard across our laps. I could see tears falling on the white notes. I held her hand underneath them. After they broke up, I started going to see her whenever Marc was at judo. She gave it up to me on the second try, and I was boning her on a regular basis by the time they got back together. She was such a good lay, because in the sack she's just like she is in life, she puts up a fight. She pushes back.

Marc and Coney were always making out in front of me. It kind of killed me and I asked her to choose. She knew I was so into her, and Marc was fucking all those other girls. Of course she chose him, and I kept seeing her. For this I didn't hold her quite as guilty as me. She was leveling things out, while I was tipping a scale that could never be righted. My brother is one blackhearted, amoral fucker, but he would never do anything like that to me. I used to wonder what was in it for Coney. Why bother cheating on Marc with someone who looked exactly like him? It just seemed like double the work. Now, I think she was trying to make one person out of the two: the one she loved and the one who loved her.

One night on the way to the movies, Coney ran a red light and we ploughed into the side of another car. Marc and I were sitting in the back and we were okay, but Coney's forehead was split open. You could see bone. Her teeth were clacking and her lips were white. Marc phoned for help, and Richie Bauer, from the grade above, limped over and said he thought his mother was dead. Coney became hysterical. She started crying and saying all kinds of shit. When she began making sense, I realized she was confessing her sins. I covered my eyes and prayed she'd skip the one about us.

When the words came out of her mouth, Marc picked me up by my clothes and dragged me away from the car, to the edge of the road. He asked me if it was true and I said yes. He started beating my face in. I threw punches and managed to land a few, but Marc spent his weekday afternoons training to hit and to be hit. I knew I was fucked. When Richie tried to help me out, Marc split his lip and went back to decking me. I could feel bones crack. The paramedics arrived and pulled him off me. I couldn't see for a couple of hours, and I ate through a straw for a month. The only good thing was this bone in my nose didn't fuse properly, so I had to have it rebroken and reset a few times. Now you can tell us apart. For the rest of high school, people called me Picasso. I took up drawing and painting so it would seem like they were complimenting the art.

My brother had fractured Richie's jaw. He got two hundred hours of community service and my parents had to pay a fine. Mrs Bauer survived. She'd been an amateur marathon runner, and now she would walk with a stick. Coney had a rail of stitches and went to juvie. Her license was suspended for a year. She came back with a long, puffy scar bisecting her forehead, and something fierce and glittery that hadn't been there before.

Coney used to cane it harder than both of us put together, but after the accident, she couldn't drink without getting a headache, and she could only do a little bit of drugs. For her seventeenth birthday we did microdots. Coney got a nosebleed and then she blacked out. We were still finding the balls to dial 911 when she came to. We checked for brain damage by asking her sums and quizzing her general knowledge. She knew the answers, but she stuttered when she spoke. When we asked her what the date was, she said a year a few years ago. She asked me what had happened to my nose. Marc and I locked eyes. We'd found the reset button. He raised an eyebrow and I nodded. He told a story of how we'd gotten into it with some guys from another school in the parking lot behind the cinema.

After this, Marc and I were golden. If things had been reversed, it wouldn't have been enough for me. I guess I'd care more about losing his respect than hers. I sometimes thought that even though Coney didn't remember, her body did. I felt it in the way she arranged herself around me. I was still bent up about her and she had no idea, so she was always toeing that line, but I'd been given the chance to start over and I took it seriously. Marc and Coney were better this time. He was the same, he just didn't rub it in her face as much.

It was senior year and Coney had forgotten everything

she'd learned in high school. The stutter didn't go away, and she lost her place on the debate team. When her GPA plummeted, her parents hired a tutor and forced Coney to drop out of the band. We didn't see her much after that. At Christmas, we found out Coney's mom had had an affair with our dad. It blew our minds. You never suspected old people were up to anything. I was just glad they hadn't hit it off and turned us all into a Greek myth.

That was when Coney's family moved upstate. Marc hadn't found anyone good enough to replace her, so he turned DD-MM-YY into a concept band, recording the drum and synth parts as a guy with sandy hair, and the vocals in full drag. He Photoshopped the band pictures. When he gigged he sang in drag and I played the synth in sunglasses, pretending to be him. I still talked to Coney on the phone every day. Last spring when Marc and I were raking in college acceptance letters, Coney found out she would have to repeat the last year of high school. In the summer, Marc graduated as class valedictorian. I haven't spoken to Coney since I started art school in the fall.

The pills haven't taken. I go to the living room to pour myself a scotch. When I drink it, they finally hit. My bones blush and a thudding cloud expands in my head. I refill the glass before going to my room and clicking on the desk lamp. Coney flips onto her back and her body comes out of the sheets. She's wearing a tank top and underpants. The ribbed cotton is stretched thinner across her tear-shaped tits and her nipples show through. I stand there staring at her like a loser pervert. I haven't been laid in forever. Art school is crawling with horny, experimental girls, but the only ones who want to get with me are two-baggers. And I'm never smart enough to look at them and know that. I always have to test it out in a way that's humiliating for us both.

You wouldn't think a nose would be such a big deal, but apparently it is. I read somewhere that it reminds people of your cock, so maybe it's like bad advertising or something. I mean, it's the only difference between Marc and me, and he's always up to his eyebrows in pussy. I only ever get it when I'm back here for the holidays. The girls here know how I'm supposed to look. If I went to Galen's right now, I could have my dick in someone by midnight, easy. The crazy thing is, I'd rather get a bottle of lotion and jack off and think about Coney. I wonder if Marc is done with her. She opens her eyes and blinks at me. Her hair sticks to her cheeks and her makeup's clotted.

"Come here you little bitch," she says, her hard, wet eyes slipping.

I don't know who she thinks I am. I set the glass on the nightstand and take off my T-shirt. I climb into the fever bed, pressing up against her and breathing in that coolant-like scent that emanates from people's skin when they're fucked up and you're not. I pull back to look at her. Her eyes are closed and her breathing's deep and even. Her mascara's flaking off and there are black crumbs on her cheeks. She's put concealer on the scar but you can still see the raised surface. I push on my boner and roll onto my back.

Now and then, Coney would tell us she'd recovered the missing swatch of memory. Marc and I would start sweating bullets, and she'd describe three years in the life of a Tunisian goat herder, Tokyo elevator girl or favela capo in Rio. It was as if the missing time had been replaced by a collective memory of what everyone in the world had been doing those three years. Not all the memories belonged to people. There had been a giant sea turtle, and a Paris schoolgirl's satchel. At times I wondered if it was an elaborate joke. If it was, I thought it was beautiful, and I admired the research.

"Adam?" Her voice sounds like cotton candy. "What are you doing here?"

"I live here."

She smiles and hugs me. I wonder if she thought she was dreaming earlier.

"How've you been?" I say, keeping the lower half of my body away.

"Good. I gg-graduated."

"Congrats." I sit up, fluffing the blanket, and reach for the glass.

I take a sip before offering it to her. She props herself on her elbow and I can see sideboob as she downs it in one. We both turn as a Siamese cat slinks into the room. It's wearing a black collar studded with blinking blue LEDs. The lights stop when the cat stands still. It meows loudly, showing its fangs. Its eyes glow in a spooky way.

"Aw," Coney says.

The cat turns and leaves, the lights flashing.

"I've never seen that cat before in my life," I tell her.

"Oh," she says, chewing her mouth. "You saw it too?" She lies back down and sets the glass on the bed.

I move it to the nightstand. "Have you had any new memories?"

"Uh-huh," she says softly, "it was bizarre. I was in love with a mm-musician who was fucking around on me."

I look at her.

"I was fucking his brother. We were all as bad as each other."

Shit. "When did you remember?"

"Marc told me."

"When?"

"He didn't mean to."

"Tonight?"

"I mean, fuck," she says. "You're supposed to be better than him."

I was about to apologize, but now I just want to punch something. I look at my knuckles. "Don't compare us. We're nothing alike."

"The difference is, you screw people over to get what you want."

"Great," I say. "Thanks."

"You're selfish, but least you want something. Marc doesn't want anything. He just wants to win."

I can feel her looking at me, but I can't look at her.

"Adam," she says and starts bawling.

I don't know what to do. The sound comes from deep inside her. I get up and find my T-shirt and give it to her. She sits up and blows her nose. We sit, not looking at each other. Every now and then, she hiccups.

"Was this one of your sick games with your brother," she says in a thick voice, "or did you want *me*?"

"You," I say, getting hard again.

"Don't lie."

"I was crazy about you."

"Oh. He didn't tell me that."

"He doesn't know. He probably thinks it was all about him."

"Did I know?"

I nod.

"Then why didn't I pick you?"

"I don't know."

She looks at my tented jeans. "Were we any good?"

I lean over and start kissing and biting her neck. I tongue her mouth, cupping her breasts through her shirt. She makes small sounds and her nipples knot under the cotton. She pushes me back onto the pillows and straddles me, pulling off her top. I just look at her for a minute. I'd forgotten how beautiful. She unbuttons my jeans and takes me out. She holds me in both hands, circling the tip with her thumb.

"Unh," I say, "think it's okay?"

She doesn't answer, she just rubs the pre-come around. I sit up and push her tits together and lick them. I lift one, and bite and suck the underboob the way she likes. She wriggles down under the blankets and pulls off my jeans and skivvies. I lie back and her hair tickles my stomach, her mouth wrapping over me. I'd forgotten this about her: she has the smallest, hottest mouth, as if she's storing lava in her cheeks. I shut my eyes, holding her hair by the roots. My bones start to liquefy.

When I'm about to come, I flip her onto her back and take off her underwear. I roll her nipple on my tongue and rub her clit with my thumb until her lips get slippery. I glide my middle finger in and out, then fold her legs up and push in. God. It's like sticking your cock into the sun. I fuck her deep and slow, watching her mouth and feeling her move. When I get too close, I pull out and let my dick cool. She pushes me off and climbs on top of me. She straddles my ribs and puts her breasts on my face, squeezing them together so I can't breathe. I see television static and my cock starts throbbing. I spurt a little and I'm just about to shoot my wad when she releases me and I get an oxygen rush that stops it. She fits her pussy snugly over my cock and I almost lose it again. I grab her hips and hold her still for a second. Her cunt feels warm and muscular. She rocks back and forth, her breasts swaying and knocking together. Her pussy tightens and the flesh around her bellybutton quivers when she gets close. She comes and comes, waves of hot silk—I grit my teeth and push her off. I bend her over and really give it to her. Our skin smacks and she arches her back, tipping her ass up so it looks fucking peachy, and I can feel a ridge of muscle or bone across the top of my dick and she squeezes—I pull out and stroke it, rubbing the head against her ass cheek, my body buckling as I squirt up her back.

Hollowed out, we fall onto the bed and zone out for a while. Coney doesn't turn around. I find the snotty T-shirt and use a clean part to wipe her back and hair. I should have worn a rubber. Marc and I are monozygotic, so if one of us ever knocks her up, we'll never find out which one it was.

"Are you back together?" I say.

"I haven't fucked him, if that's what you're asking."

I don't think she's a liar, but I don't believe her. I just can't imagine her saying no to him. "Still. We probably shouldn't say anything."

"I wasn't planning to," she says.

She turns over and I rest my head on her tit. Her heart's ticking like a drum machine.

"Your pulse is too fast," I tell her. "What are you on?"

"I kittyflipped. You?"

"Nothing." My tongue feels swollen. "A couple of dolls."

We get out of bed and look for our clothes. When I bend down to pull a shirt from the drawer, the Seconal washes over my head in a wave. Getting dressed, I can hear fabric rustling and carpet fibers crunching underfoot.

"Sorry I fell off the map," Coney says, zipping her skirt. It sounds like a passing car. "I just needed to get through the year."

"Don't worry about it."

Her bangles chime when she slips them on. I rub my face in case there's makeup on it and we get back under the covers. The bed starts to sway.

"Adam." She sounds like she's underwater.

I open my eyes.

"I'm scared of the future."

I stretch and look at her. "But you've caught up now. You're all set."

"I need more time in high school. I tried to flunk out at the last minute."

"No one remembers half of it. I'm sure you've come out even."

"I feel like a fruit you cut open to find it's rotten inside." She lays her head on my chest. "I'm just not ready for life, the way I used to be. Something's wiped the specialness out of me."

"What are you talking about? You're the most special person I know."

"I'm not," she says. "I used to be. When I was little, I could always feel the promise of it, like a tooth. A germ that would develop into something no one in the world has ever seen before. It's not there anymore."

"You're just depressed. It'll come back. And you're great without having to do anything. Just doing fuck-all with you feels like the best thing I've ever done. Maybe the germ is gone because it's already propagated. Maybe it's you. Maybe you're that astonishing, heart-stopping thing."

"No," she says.

We're quiet for a while.

"We're all scared," I tell her. "I mean, nobody's not scared. But that's part of it, you know?"

She moves her head to the pillow and blinks at me.

"You'll be great," I say. "But hey, take it easy out there, okay?"

"I know." She smiles, showing little teeth, so sharp they're see-through at the tips. I hold her hand under the blankets as she starts to duck out.

"Wake up, virgin."

The overhead light's in my eyes and my brother's sitting on my chest, holding a bong. I push him off. Coney's rolled in a ball at the far edge of the bed. Marc kneels on the carpet and puts the bong to his mouth, covering the carb and lighting the bowl. The water bubbles and the piney, velvety stink fills the room.

"Dude," I croak. "She's asleep, you fuck."

He clears the cylinder with one breath and holds the hit like he's suppressing a laugh. Clouds bleed from his mouth.

"What time is it?"

"Time to do a hit." He shoves the bong in my face.

I sit up and look at the clock on my desk. I lie back down.

"Can you fuck off," I say, "and turn out the light?"

He comes over and starts jabbing me in the ribs. I swing at him, trying not to shake the bed. I get up and shove him and he takes a quick step back, knocking the lamp off the desk. I cover Coney with the blanket and turn off the overhead light. I step into the hall, and when Marc comes out I pull the door shut behind him. I leave him standing there and go to my parents' bathroom to take a slash. I hold my dick, watching the beam of piss. I swallow another doll and go into their room. I flop on Dad's side of the bed. I can feel the shape of his body in the mattress.

It's so weird to think that every man in our family has

fucked a woman in their family. It kind of makes you wonder. If it was just about sex, we could have picked anyone. There must have been something each family had that the other family needed. Can families fall in love, like the opposite of a feud, and why isn't there a name for it? Maybe it's called *before the feud*. Marc comes in and sits on the carpet, his eyes shining like dimes. He hits the bong, and I notice he's switched out the water for mouthwash and ice cubes.

Marc's pre-med. He's planning to be a plastic surgeon. He says he wants to fix my nose, but I think he just wants to cut people up. Either way, he knows I'd never let him anywhere near me with a scalpel. I wouldn't need his help anyway. My parents offer me a nose job every Christmas and birthday. They're incredibly superficial, considering how clapped-out they both are. It's no wonder Marc and I turned out the way we have. We're the embodiment of their vanity. Sometimes I even think the triplet thing might have been down to eugenics. *You need your face*, my mother says, as if I haven't got one at the moment. I'll never get it fixed. It might be the ball-ache of my life, but it's mine.

Marc taps the ashes into the wastebasket, replaces the bowl, and passes me the bong. He pulls a baggie out of his pocket and tosses it on the bed. I start to pack a bowl.

"You should've come to Galen's," he says, setting the lighter on the pillow. "She has this hot Swiss girl over. Slamming body, like *wa-pow*. Tits up to her chin. Pierced tongue." He stretches out on the carpet.

"And let me guess, you porked her. Fascinating." I take a hit and hold it. The peppermint scalds my sinuses. Coughing, I hand him the bong. He pulls a deformed paperclip from his jeans pocket and pokes the contents of the bowl before lighting it.

"She's definitely worth a squirt," he says, talking through the hit. "But get this, she's Galen's girlfriend." He blows out the smoke.

"Fuu—. That's hot."

"At college this girl is known as Flipper."

"Um, because she has an incredibly large vagina?"

"No you moron. She flips girls." He offers me the bong. I shake my head and lie back, seeing Coney's body projected on the ceiling. I think about her cool, slippery skin, and her warm insides.

"Hey, queef breath," Marc says, "did they buy a cat?"

I turn. It's sitting in the doorway, cleaning its paws. The blue lights twinkle.

"It's like a scary robot cat."

"I don't like it either."

The cat rearranges itself so we can see its balls.

"What's up with telling Coney we lied?" I say. "Oh, and a heads-up would have been nice."

He doesn't answer.

"Whatever. She's done with you, bro."

"Thanks for the news flash, Friend Zone."

"She's kind of falling apart, you know."

Marc looks at me. He gets up and comes to the edge of the bed. "You fucked her, didn't you?"

He widens his stance and I start to block my face, but then his body language tessellates with the way he's been acting all night, and I know. Coney wasn't lying. She really did knock him back. I drop my guard and stand up. I get right in his face, close enough to kiss. When our noses touch, he steps back and his eyes remind me of when you look into an animal's eyes and it seems intelligent. He turns and leaves the room. My brother is a destroyer. Nothing survives. Only me, and I have to wonder what that means. It feels like the loneliest thing in the world.

I hear a sound. It's soft, and deep. I go out into the hall. My bedroom door is open and there's a low glow coming from the lamp on the floor. I hear it again: halfway between a sex noise and a sob, but muffled. An image flashes through my mind like dark lightning and something uncoils inside me. I run down the hall.

Coney's lying on her back, staring up at the ceiling, and Marc is hugging her legs with his face pushed into her stomach. That's how they always make up, except this time it's my brother who's crying. He lifts his head and looks at me, his face wet and different. When our eyes meet, the world moves half a turn, and the picture in front of me changes. I stumble forward, trying to find the edge of the bed behind the image of Coney standing beside our pool, lacing her hair into a messy plait. Three chlorine-tinted bales, locked around one another and tied off with a rubber band.

Laurens

B oth have boys' names for surnames and live off Interstate 10 in towns that have girls' names. They have bloody Popsicle mouths and uncombed filament hair. They smell like butter and jelly. They know how to skin things. Their fathers are hunters.

The summer their mothers suicided, the Laurens went to SeaWorld San Diego, where they occupied the same quadrant of the bleachers during the Shamu show, their screams mingling. The girl Lauren nibbled a churro in the background of a photo of the boy Lauren stroking a manta ray. Hotel beds were icy and bright, the fathers' eye sockets smeared with sunburn.

They wrap scarred knees over monkey bars and dangle upside down, spilt hair ablaze in sunlight, the knowledge of pain stashed like candy in the cheek. They're as hard and as pretty as baby teeth, and people always say they are growing, but the Laurens don't think so. They are pencils, getting smaller and sharper.

Totally Hair Barbie has white-blond hair reaching all the way down to her toes. Lauren holds the legs while Kumi braids the hair. Kumi has slippery black bangs and pierced ears with aqua stones and she's a really good braider. When she's done she fastens the end with a clip. Lauren nods. It looks perfect. Kumi unsnaps the clip and combs out the hair with her fingers. "You do it."

She holds the legs so Lauren can braid, but Lauren doesn't know how, so she twists the hair around and around into a ball and wraps an elastic band over it. It looks retarded.

"That looks cool," Kumi says, kneeling up and prancing Barbie along the windowsill. "Don't you think she seems sort of French?"

Lauren smiles. Every girl in her class knows she's here tonight. Lately she plays a game where she pretends she's on a TV show. She starts the camera in the morning when she's running down the slope from her house, and switches it off in the afternoon when the school bus spits her out onto the curb. This way only the good stuff gets on the tape. Today Kumi's mom picked them up from school, so Lauren didn't have to stop filming. It's a special all-night episode. Kumi passes her the Barbie. Lauren holds the legs and watches Kumi's fingers flutter.

"When are you going to invite me to your house?" Kumi says. "I can come—not next weekend, but the weekend after."

"He doesn't let me have anyone over."

Kumi laughs. It sounds like a coin in a can. "Are you serious?"

"I know."

"Really?" Kumi says. "Never?"

"I hate him. I'm leaving the second I turn fifteen."

Kumi looks up, surprised. "It's no big deal. We can hang out here." She wraps a ponytail holder around the end of the braid. "Want me to do it on you?"

Lauren nods and Kumi scoots closer.

"Your hair's the exact same color as Barbie's but it feels different," Kumi says, working out the tangles, "it's thicker and rougher."

Lauren scratches her palms. She gets nervous when people talk about how she looks, even before they've said anything mean. Kids at school call her Lizard because she gets eczema really bad sometimes, and because of her eyes. They're greeny yellow and too wide apart.

"It'll get more soft and shiny when you grow up," Kumi says. Her breath smells like hot juice.

Lauren sits very still as Kumi braids her hair. She's allowed to erase things from the tape, so she wipes the part where she told Kumi about the secret plan. She has to blink in a special way to make it work. She starts to think about Cody who used to work at the drugstore, who always had a shiner and was so pale he was almost see-through. One day he had one of those big casts around his neck and then he disappeared. Everyone thought he was buried in his father's garden until they saw him dancing in a music video.

"All done," Kumi says.

Lauren touches the braid.

"What do you want to do now?"

Lauren shrugs.

Kumi shrugs back. "Hide and seek?"

"Nuh-uh. I hate that game."

"Why do you hate it?"

"Why do you like it?"

"It's fun."

Lauren pulls a face. "How can you think that?"

"You're being weird," Kumi says.

Maybe Kumi isn't talking about the real hide-and-seek. Maybe there's a funny pretend version that girls play together. Lauren's not quite sure she'd want to play that game either, but if Kumi gives a good report on Monday, more friends and invites will follow. Lauren has to live with him for seven more years. If she can spend every Friday night at other people's houses, that's like being away for one year out of the seven.

"I'll play," she says, "but I want to be the boy."

Kumi scrunches her nose. "What do you mean, the boy?"

"The seeker."

"Yah, fine." Kumi gets up and walks out of the room. "Count to fifty," she calls from the doorway, "no, a hundred!" She runs down the hall.

Lauren chews a cuticle and looks around. Kumi's house is nice and it smells nice. The furniture is velvety and seems to sigh when you sit on it. Kumi's walls are light purple and covered in artwork and stickers, and her bed is a bunk bed, except it's double-wide. They can both fit up there and Lauren can hardly wait. Where the lower bunk would normally be is a desk with a computer and printer, as if Kumi is a business-woman or something. Maybe it's better that Kumi can never come over. She might not understand why Lauren doesn't have a bedroom door. He made it into a coffee table. It still has the doorknob. He uses it to store elastic bands.

She goes to look for Kumi. The hallway's cool and dim, with a glossy wood floor. She sock-skates past the den where Kumi's parents are watching TV. Kumi's mom is plump and cozy with a large beautiful face and Kumi's dad is a braces dentist. She switches on the light in the bathroom and looks inside the towel cupboard and behind the shower door. Out in the hall are some family photos on the wall. Each one is lit by a thin silver lamp. In the pictures Kumi gets bigger while her mother's hair gets shorter.

Kumi's parents' door is open. Lauren goes in and clicks on the overhead light. There are long purple drapes and an enormous bed with lamps sticking out of the headboard. When she gets down on her stomach to peek under the bed, the floorboards stick to her hands like the pages of a magazine. She gets up and goes to the window, finds the gap in the curtains and pokes her head through.

Kumi's standing there with smiley eyes and both hands over her mouth. Lauren goes behind the curtain and tickles her. Kumi squeals and wriggles. Her eyes get bigger as Lauren backs her up against the window and lifts up her dress. When Lauren tries to put her hand in Kumi's underwear, Kumi slugs her. Lauren stumbles backwards, getting caught on the curtain. It holds her for a second before the rings snap. She falls and Kumi and the curtain fall on top of her. It happens too slow and too fast, like a nightmare.

They're unwrapping themselves when Kumi's mom comes running into the room.

"Look what you've done!" she scolds. She yells something in Japanese.

Kumi starts to cry. Lauren wonders how long it will take to walk home. His shift will have started by now, but she knows how to force the screen door and wriggle through the cat flap. The freeway will be dark.

Kumi's father comes in and frowns at the curtain on the floor. His hair is very neat and Lauren cringes at how disgusted he's going to be when Kumi tells him what happened, but Kumi just stands there, bawling her eyes out. Her parents speak to one another quietly in Japanese and walk around picking up the broken curtain rings. They're as calm as people on TV, and the way Kumi's overreacting makes Lauren want to punch her.

Kumi's father smiles at Lauren in an embarrassed way, saying, "Kumi-chang, that's enough now."

Kumi nods and hiccups. She wipes her nose with the shoulder of her dress and skulks out of the room. Her parents pick up the curtain and start to fold it.

"I'm sorry," Lauren tells them.

"It's okay, no problem," Kumi's mom says.

Lauren goes out into the hall. She fetches toilet paper from the bathroom and goes to Kumi's room. Kumi's sitting at her desk, breathing weirdly. Her shoulders are jerking. Lauren hands her the tissue and sits on the carpet.

Kumi blows her nose. "Haven't you ever played hide-and-seek before?"

"Sure I have." Lauren gets a feeling like when you haven't finished blowing up a balloon and you let go. The way it whizzes around hitting everything.

"That's not how you play, dummy." Kumi's eyes are red and ugly.

"Shut up," Lauren says.

Kumi folds her arms and swivels her chair to face the other way. Lauren touches the handles of the desk drawers. She blinks her eyes and erases the tape.

She lies on her side with her forehead pressed to the slats of the bunk, listening to the catch in Kumi's breathing. After the fight, Kumi didn't laugh or smile anymore, and she fell asleep halfway through their game of Othello. She hadn't eaten even half the candy in her pillowcase. When Lauren tried to wake her up, she rolled to the wall. Lauren switched off the torch and ate the rest of the candy in the dark. It tasted like metal.

Sugar from the gummy worms grits the sheets. The solar system shines on the far wall. Lauren loves planets. She loves their names and their magnetism and the way their orbits look like bangles. When she grows up she wants to have three jobs: she'll be an open-heart surgeon in the morning so she won't make any mistakes, an inventor in the afternoon because that's when she has her best ideas, and an astronaut at night. She'll go to college first, to learn how to take rock samples. Lauren wants to go to Venus because it's the hottest world. She'll have a special suit made, the same as people wear in the movies when they're set on fire. Everybody goes to the moon.

The door opens. She shuts her eyes and light washes over the lids. Kumi's mom moves the blankets and tucks Lauren in a bit tighter. She smells like pink lotion. Her nightgown swishes and the door clicks shut. Earlier, she brushed Lauren's teeth for her. It was kind of weird, but Lauren liked the way she'd held her by the back of the head and afterwards her teeth felt so smooth.

Lauren's mom didn't go to college, she went to LA. Later she came back and married Lauren's dad. She liked to say she wasn't city-beautiful and had found out the hard way. She used to stare through the TV, touching her mouth. Sometimes she walked in fashion shows at the mall. She had freckles in the morning when Lauren crawled into her bed. On the last night, she lay on Lauren's carpet doing stretching exercises. Since she's been gone, candy tastes bad. Rain falls harder and darkness is darker.

The friendship is over. Kumi knows that Lauren is awful. She'll tell everyone at school. Lauren thinks of an apple. It's pretty okay inside. It only starts to turn rotten when you cut it open and it touches the world.

She's still awake when the planets on the wall stop glowing.

The car stops in front of the house. Lauren unclips the seatbelt and looks in the rearview mirror. Kumi's in the backseat in her ballet clothes, looking out the window.

"Thank you, and sorry," Lauren says to Kumi's mom.

"Don't be silly." Kumi's mom smiles. "We loved having you." She makes the locks on the doors pop up.

Blinking her eyes to stop the camera, Lauren gets out and shuts the door. It's a hot, dark day. The sky has berry-red lines, as if it's been scratched.

Kumi waves. "See you Monday!"

"Goodbye," Lauren says.

The car turns around, kicking up rocks and dirt. It bounces down the track. She watches it fade, the dust rising.

His truck is here and the screen door's open. If there's no girl, he'll sleep until dark. The girls come from work. Some of them do weird and desperate things the first time they meet her, like baking banana bread or trying to teach her to knit. They stop when they realize it makes no difference to him. Leaving her shoes on the porch, she goes in with sock feet.

The house is dark and stuffy. The living room shades are down and the TV's fizzing cartoons. His door is shut and there's no guitar music, no blade of light underneath. A glass on the coffee table holds a bunch of cigarette butts. She picks up the glass, turning it to see if any of the filters have lipstick prints. The girl who doesn't wear lipstick eats Skittles nonstop. She goes to the kitchen and pokes through the top layer of the trash. There's no Skittles packet.

The cartoons are spinning and popping. She finds the remote and turns down the sound. She pads over to his door and cups her ear to it. No voices, so she opens it and pokes her head around. He's alone and asleep. She shuts the door and goes to the kitchen, gets the Tupperware from the freezer and peels off the lid. AccuTip saboted slugs are the best, and green and gold are her favorite colors. She counts out five shells, stuffs them in her shorts pockets and puts the Tupperware back. Her hands are sweating.

Under the pennies and screws and bits of uncooked spaghetti in the drawer under the microwave is the key on its loop of wire. She goes to the living room and unlocks the cupboard by the TV. Behind the fly rods, the guns are stored open and safe. She lifts out the Persuader, making sure the red dot isn't visible on top of the receiver. When she pushes the slide forward to close the chamber, it clatters. She'll have to pump it again to chamber the first shell and she doesn't want him to hear, so she slings the gun on her back, hooking her thumb through the strap, and heads outside.

The Persuader feels heavy and unfamiliar. The .22 is the one she knows, the one she learned on, and fits her body perfect, but it's more for snakes and squirrels and the smoothbore barrel works better with the Heavy Dove Loads. He told her never to fire AccuTips through it because they'll keyhole. That means the shell turns sideways and you don't get a clean shot.

The screen door bangs shut behind her. It's a little cooler outside, but muggy. The sky looks thick and white, and this all starts to feel like something that happened so long ago she can barely remember it. She could lie down and go to sleep, and it would still keep happening without her. Wind shakes the trees. A cool bead of sweat slides down her cheek and into her mouth. The taste of salt when she swallows tugs her back into her body. Kneeling on the porch, she digs the shells from her pockets and checks the safety again. She holds down the loading gate and feeds the slugs into the magazine tube. The spring makes a clipping sound as she pops them in.

She stands up, presses the slide release and pumps the action. The sound makes her heart touch her ribs. She carries the shotgun into the house, catching the screen door with her shoulder so it doesn't slam. Colored light from the TV flashes against the sofa cushions as she walks through the living room. She wipes her hand against her shorts before turning the door handle. The hinge squeaks as she eases the door open. She slides the safety forward, grips the gun with both hands and tries to breathe. Finger on the trigger guard, she raises the shotgun and steps around the door.

He's sleeping on his side, clutching the sheet with a fist, breathing shallow and regular. She moves towards him through bars of sunlight, stepping over grayish twists of cloth. There's a smell of wet fur. His head is off the pillow, on his bent arm. She stands by the bed with her cheek smushed against the side of the buttstock and peers down the rib at the centre of his forehead. As she dips the muzzle, training the bead on the space between his eyes, the picture turns white and grainy and she sees herself standing, holding the shotgun.

She sees herself walking backwards out of the room and closing the door. Unloading the shells one by one. Leaning the gun against the back of the closet and locking it. Returning the key to its drawer. She can undo everything she's done so far, and she'll still have something she didn't have before. She can put the shells in the freezer and watch cartoons, and every time she looks at the cupboard by the TV, she'll remember how this feels.

His warmth comes through the sheet. His turned-earth smell of smoke and skin. She slips three fingers under the guard and squeezes the trigger. The top of his head bursts, spraying blood and bone straight up the wall. Pillow stuffing floats down. She hears the casing whirring across the floor. There are brains. He flops like a fish, making dull sounds. She pumps the slide, finds his chest, and fires. His body opens like a flower. A blackish circle keeps getting bigger. Her T-shirt sticks to her skin as she walks to the phone, and she starts to feel the burn from the recoil.

Katy, Texas

Lauren's left tooth in front is so wobbly, it swings all the way out like a cat flap. He shows Jericho, who always knows what to do.

"We have to tie it to the doorknob with dental floss," Jericho says with his mouth full. He has frizzy brown hair and more freckles than skin. "I'll slam it for you."

"Does it hurt?"

"Nah. But it bleeds forever."

Lauren pulls a face. "No thanks."

"Wuss."

He slept over at Jericho's last night, like he does every Friday. In the morning they had toaster waffles with sliced Prosage Roll instead of breakfast sausage, and Stripples, which are Christian bacon with perfect pink and yellow stripes. Their food is weird but Lauren likes it because he's funny about meat. He doesn't mind skinning deer and rabbits with his dad, but eating them is another thing. He borrowed one of Jericho's clip-on bow-ties and they went to Sabbath School and church.

Lauren's been Saved since the first grade. It's a secret from his dad, who's kind of touchy about God. He's just jealous because he's an atheist, which is a heathen religion with not such good stories. When Lauren had been to Sabbath School ten times in a row, the teacher gave Jericho a pencil and a gold star. She said he gets a crown in heaven, too. Lauren thought since Jericho had already won all the prizes, maybe it was time to stop going, but it turns out he's supposed to keep going till he dies because later God is planning to look it up in his chart. Religion is scary at times, like when the preacher's face gets red and everybody cries, but Lauren loves the magazines and potlucks, and stories with Fuzzy Felts. Most of all he loves being Saved, like a piece of chewing gum that's still perfectly fine, stuck to God's bedpost.

After church, Jericho's dad barbecued FriPats and Leanies out on the deck, and Jericho's mom made ice-cream sundaes. Jericho's parents went to have their nap and Jericho and Lauren made a huge fort in the living room. They used chairs and cushions from every room in the house and even some of the books. When Lauren went to get more cushions from the den, he heard Jericho's parents making strange sounds and running around inside their room. It spooked him and he's ready to go home. Dad normally comes in the afternoon but today Lauren was still here for vespers and bath time, and now they're having dinner and he still hasn't shown up.

Jericho's dad is a doctor-on-call and they called him today, so they're eating without him. Jericho's mom has bright yellow hair that's black in the parting. She made spaghetti with Tender Bits and when she goes to answer the phone, Jericho and Lauren do the special trick. They swallow a strand of spaghetti without chewing, keeping hold of the end, and they pull it out. The noodle comes out clean. It makes you gag but it's worth it.

When Jericho's mom comes back from the phone, she puts her chin on her hand and stares out the window at the driveway. She's been in a funny mood all evening, like when they showed her the fort, she wasn't as impressed as they thought she'd be. When Lauren and Jericho are done eating, she switches on the pool lights and sends them out onto the deck to play. They pretend they're in a SWAT team with M16s and bazookas. Jericho's parents don't allow any guns in the house, not even pretend ones that's just a finger and thumb and them saying *pyoom pyoom*. Lauren's dad says Jericho's parents don't have a grip on reality.

Lauren's dad lets him be around when he's cleaning his guns. Sometimes he shows Lauren how to undo the catch on the smallest one and how to hold it, in case he ever needs to threaten a burglar. Lauren hopes he won't and hopes he will. Dad says the burglar will get scared and run, but if he doesn't, to shoot him in the thigh. Only to maim and never to kill. Never the head or the heart.

Jericho knows about the guns and bugs Lauren to let him see them, but his parents never let him go to Lauren's. Sometimes Lauren wonders if it's better to be like him and Dad and have a gun and reality, or to be like Jericho's family with no gun and no reality, but a house with a pool and God and Jericho's mom there. Maybe some people have all those things and for them life is perfect.

They go inside to play golf in the den. Tonight it seems obvious that the golf course is just a fake grass mat with three holes. It's really not that much fun without Jericho's dad giving them tips on their putting style and patting their shoulders when they do it right. Sometimes he gives them some bourbon in a tiny glass. He would like them to get some hair on their chests.

Dad still hasn't shown up when Jericho's bedtime comes, so Jericho's mom gets them both ready for bed. Putting his pajamas on again makes Lauren sad. It seems like his dad has forgotten about him. When Jericho's mom prays, Lauren and Jericho open their eyes and watch her. It's like she's sleep-talking. She tucks them in and gives Lauren a hug and a kiss. She leaves the night-light on. Jericho has some Israelites hidden inside his pillowcase and they have a few whispered battles before Jericho crashes out.

Lauren never feels all that sleepy here. He lays on his side and wiggles his tooth, listening to Jericho's breathing that sounds like a broken machine. He wishes he had Spiderman pajamas like Jericho's. He likes the trundle bed where he's lying, the way it slides out already made up from under Jericho's bed. If he sank much deeper down into the mattress and lay very flat, you could push him back in just like closing a drawer, and he'd be safe as anything.

That chiming sound means the car door's open, but Lauren's pretty sure he's in the trundle bed at Jericho's. When he lifts his head, he feels his cheek unstick from the leather seat. There's black sky in the windscreen, stars winking like staples, and the perfume tree hanging from the rearview mirror. He's in the backseat of his dad's car parked behind the ABC. Lauren likes it when people take you somewhere when you're asleep. It seems magical. He decides to look for his dad in the store.

When he climbs out and shuts the door, he notices he's barefoot and in his pajamas. The air is as warm as dog breath.

He can still hear the chimes so he goes around to the driver's side and opens and closes the door. As he walks across the lot, he feels day-old sunshine trapped in the asphalt.

The mat in front of the store is scratchy. The doors swish open. Inside, the floor feels clammy and there are bright reflections painted on the windows. The cashier is trying to sleep on the counter. She has pink hair and thin arms decorated with tattoos. A fan on a chair swings its head from side to side like it's dancing and concentrating. Lauren sees his dad over by the fridges. Lauren smiles and waves, but his dad doesn't notice, so Lauren gets kind of mad and decides not to go over. The cashier lifts her head and blinks. She seems young, like a babysitter. He smiles, feeling shy.

"Look," he says, wiggling his tooth.

She yawns and smiles. He looks at the sea-black dragon and purple octopus twisted around her arms, the mermaid peeping around the crook of her elbow.

"My mom used to have tattoos."

"She did? You mean she had them lasered off?"

He shakes his head. "She's dead. She killed herself."

The girl's mouth forms an O. "Baby," she says in a pretty way.

"It's okay," he says, "it was a long time ago. She was very sad. She cried with tissues when she watched a movie on TV."

"She sounds beautiful," the girl says.

Lauren's dad plunks his shopping basket on the counter. The girl's face changes when she looks at him. She looks at Lauren and then at Lauren's dad. "You're not driving, are you sir?"

As Dad fumbles with his wallet, the girl takes the bottles out of the basket and puts them behind the counter. Dad holds out some bills. He frowns at the shopping basket.

"Sir. Is there someone who can come pick you up?"

Dad peers at her nametag. "Listen, Anna," he says, "Anna banana." He leans across and tries to look behind the counter.

"My finger's on a button," she says. "The sheriff can be here in four minutes. I've timed it."

The squiggly vein on Dad's forehead sticks out as he grabs Lauren by the elbow and pulls him away from the counter. The glass doors slide apart, mirroring colors.

"I hope someone burns down your stupid store," he yells over his shoulder.

"I only work here on weekends," the girl says.

As they cross the parking lot, Lauren looks back and sees her peering through the store window, shading the glass with her hands. He waves but she doesn't wave back. He gets in the backseat and when he looks out the window, the girl is gone. There's just the price of applesauce felt-tipped on the glass.

"Pain in the ass." Dad twists the key and flips the headlights on.

He wraps his arm around the passenger seat and reverses out of the space. The back wheels bump against the edge of the tree island and the car goes spinning out of the lot. In the distance the town lights are as pretty as party lights. Dad passes the turn for the interstate, staying on the back roads.

Lauren looks at his reflection in the glass with tree shapes flicking across it. Last week, a lady came to their school wearing gloves and a mask as if she was allergic to children. She checked them for cooties and practically all the kids in his class had them. Dad washed Lauren's hair with special shampoo before shaving it off. The blond stubble looks sparkly in the dark window.

"So," Dad says, tipping his head back as he looks at Lauren

in the rearview mirror. He seems cheered up. "What's new?"

"I had an ice-cream sundae with fudge and smashed Oreos."

"How nice," Dad says. "They're good people."

"Uh-huh, and we made a fort. Oh, and my tooth is more wobbly, see?" Lauren bares his teeth and pushes the wobbliest one out as far as he can with his tongue.

Dad turns and grins at him. "Right on," he says.

Lauren beams and settles back in his seat.

A deer shines in the headlights. Dad cusses and swerves. When he tries to right the car it skids, knocking Lauren against the window. They slide the other way and he flies across the backseat and hits his head on the door. Dad's yelling at him and the car keeps swinging from side to side. Lauren grabs the back of the passenger seat and wraps his arms around it and the car starts to spin. He hugs as tight as he can but he's slipping, something pulls him harder than he can hold. He goes out through the back window, the top of his head breaking the glass.

There's bottom-of-the-pool slowness and starry blue-green light. Tiny suns are burning in the water and there are strawberry plants growing from between the tiles. A mermaid swims towards him, her dark hair moving like smoke. She smiles with bubbles coming out of her mouth, and her face changes into his mother's face. He tries to wave and call out, but it's a movie, or a dream he's not in. She's naked like the last time Lauren saw her, but the cuts on her arms have all closed and her tattoos have come to life. Bluebirds perch on her collarbones and roses sprout from her wrists, the petals waving.

He tastes metal. There's a whistling sound coming from his cheek and when he tries to touch it, he touches bone. He lifts his head just in time to throw up on the grass. It takes a few tries before he manages to tug in a breath. He has a headache and his lungs feel wet and every time he coughs, something snaps. He spits and wipes warm black stuff from his eyes and he's so cold. Light and metal glimmer through the long grass and he hears the engine purring. The sound is comforting.

"Dad—" Lauren's voice comes out in a wheeze, hurting his ribs. He presses them and breathes. When he tries to crawl his legs are shivery and strange, so he grabs fistfuls of the grass and drags himself towards the brightness. The blood on his PJs is thick as mud and helps him to slide. When he sees the car hood wadded like tissue, he punches his legs until he can feel them and tries to stand up. The car is tilted on the bank, pointing upwards with the motor humming like it wants to take off. As he limps towards it, his tongue catches on a gap and he realizes his tooth has come out. The door's at a weird angle and it takes all his strength to get it open.

The turn signal's ticking and there's blood on the wind-screen. His father's bunched against the driver's door, glass sprayed all over his clothes. Lauren stands there, stunned. The sound of the motor had made him think his dad would be waiting impatiently, ready to drive away. The car tilts as Lauren climbs in and the door almost slams on his fingers. He climbs over the gearbox and looks at his father's face. It's a dark mash. He can't find eyes or a mouth. It's hard to understand and the trembling car and moaning engine and gas fumes are making him dizzy and sick. He kneels on the floor and puts his head on his dad's knee to keep from passing out.

His head is pounding and his cheeks feel cold and tight. He's not sure how long he's been sitting there staring at the tiny pieces of glass stuck in his hands. Dad's face is so bloody and broken. Lauren wonders if he's dead. He holds his own wrist to check how a pulse should be. He tries to find it on his father's wrist but it's hard to feel what's going on because of the vibrations of the engine.

"We have to get him to the hospital," his mom says.

Lauren turns and there's nothing there, but he knows what he heard. Although her voice is in his head sometimes, it's only ever the shape of the sound, a colorful wavy line. This was her real voice. She always sounded like she had a sore throat. He closes his eyes.

"Doctors can jumpstart people's hearts with electricity. They can do that." Her voice is scratchy-soft. He feels her breath curl against his neck, and catches her scent of soap and skin. "He might have to wear a bandage. He'll take us out for pancakes. We'll pile them up high, and cut through the whole stack at once."

He breathes her smell again before he opens his eyes. He climbs onto his father's lap and holds the steering wheel with both hands. The headlights are on, making the smash pattern on the windscreen shine like a wet spider web.

The way the car is pushed against the bank, it seems like it drove across the field by itself and got stuck trying to go uphill. Lauren looks at the gearstick. D is for Drive, so that's probably good, and the engine's chugging, so he doesn't have to turn the key. His feet don't reach the pedals unless he stands up and points his toes. He presses the left pedal and nothing happens, so he presses the right one. The car starts to creep forward, up the bank.

The long yellow grass parts like hair in the headlights. As the ground flattens out, the car goes faster. This is okay. He eases up on the pedal and peers through the cracked glass, making a circle back towards the bank. He drives down the slope and across the field. Seeing the road up ahead on the right, he steers towards it, trying to find a comfortable speed.

As the road swerves towards him, he leans on the pedal and tilts the wheel. The car skips over the ditch and sails onto the road. He's doing it. It's another thing he knows how to do, see? He grips the wheel tightly and follows the wave of the road, pressing up against it, hugging the curves. He drives down the middle, staying right on top of the two lines. His mother used to say there's a tiny train that runs along them at night. Lauren's always looking but he hasn't seen it yet. Dad has, once or twice.

Candy Glass

BLACK SCREEN
ALEXA (VOICE OVER)
Everyone calls her DC. It stands for Driverless Car, that's her specialty.

FADE IN:
A series of shots, each showing a different angle on a car that appears to be out of control. Most are night shots.

ALEXA (V.O. CONT.)
You've probably seen her: a balaclava, a pair of black gloves gripping the wheel. You may have glimpsed the whites of her eyes gleaming behind the darkened glass of a haunted Ferrari in *Demon Highway*, a scheming Bentley in the art house classic, *Legroom*. But mostly all you've seen is reflected streetlight, squirming across the windshield.

DISSOLVE TO:
MIAMI, PRESENT DAY
EXT. BIKER BAR. SUNSET.

We've arrived in Miami a month behind schedule and four million over budget. *Criminal People* has been in production for almost a year, and we have twenty days to shoot all the remaining exteriors and some of the mansion interiors. Tonight we're meant to be filming in the parking lot outside this bar. The shot takes place in LA, before my character comes to Miami, but back in LA they couldn't find a bar that looked LA enough. Theo Blatt, the director, wants to use the real biker crowd that hangs out here as background, but most of them are away at a convention, so the shoot's been postponed. I duck into the trailer, where two girls help me out of the wedding dress. One of them hands me a mirror and some face wipes. I clean off the makeup, put on my clothes, and head back outside. It's a warm spring evening and people are milling around, getting ready to head back to Miami Beach. Others drift into the bar.

INT. BIKER BAR. NIGHT.

Speed metal chugs from the speakers. I'm standing by the jukebox with Theo, who's always nervous in bars because he's a recovering alcoholic. He clenches his jaw and canes Virgin Marys the whole time. A tall, sexy woman strolls past, all messy dark-blond hair and tanned legs with a stripe of mirror sheen slicked down each shinbone. She moves with the casual stealth of the extremely fit, swathed in soft, black clothes. She's probably crew. Theo turns to see what I'm gawking at.

> THEO
> (*shouting over the music*)
> That's DC. She's one of the drivers, and she'll be taking over from Amy.

Amy's my stunt double for this picture. She couldn't come on location because we fell behind and she had another job booked. Theo feeds a dollar into the jukebox and starts flicking through the playlists. The scotch burns my throat. I want a cigarette, but I don't feel like having to talk to anyone.

DC comes back this way, eating ice cubes from a glass. Her fingers shine like sunlit metal. She has close set, silver eyes and colorless chapped lips. Her eyebrows are darker than her hair, and a touch too heavy for her face. She says hi to Theo, bumping him with her hip, and they start going over some technical stuff. Her gestures are clean and deliberate. I try to think of something clever to say, but I'm thrown by her not wanting to look at me all the time, the way most people do. Berry, the assistant director, comes over to speak with Theo. DC turns and I lean in to introduce myself, but she smiles and it throws me.

DC

People have always told me I look like you.

It's true we share more than a passing resemblance. More than is necessary. I guess she's eight, ten years younger. Women are rarely taller, but she has at least two inches on me, and her body is tighter, with smaller breasts set higher up and closer together. I can't decide whether I want to fuck her or kill her. Maybe funhouse mirrors would be scarier if, instead of making you look bad, they made you look better. She rattles the ice in her glass and scans the room over my shoulder. I freeze, trying to think of my line.

LATER

I glimpse her through the crush of people on the dance floor.

She's the only one really dancing to a song that's heavy on the drums and heroin. I move to where I can see her better.

SLOW
Her hair's in her eyes and she moves in a way that's private and beautiful, like teenage bedroom practice. I can't tell if she's lost in the music by herself or if it's a performance. I suspect it's both, and I begin to curl and blacken at the edges. She's a natural. No breathing exercises, no two Klonopin, no half a cigarette to switch it on. She's the real thing. The speakers are throbbing behind me. I feel the bass pumping out in puffs of air against my back.

DISSOLVE TO:
EXT. BEACH CONDO. THREE DAYS LATER.

I walk out of the building and down the empty sidewalk, carrying a bouquet of roses and reading the card. The street's been cordoned off and there are bright lights shining. I glance up as a car drives past with a surfboard tied to the rack. I keep reading and walking. Another car approaches, driving much faster. As it veers onto the sidewalk, I resist the urge to jump out of the way. It brakes a handspan short of me.

> THEO
> Cut. Okay guys, let's refresh the set and run it again.

Makeup comes running over. She powders my nose and sprays it with fixative. The equipment rolls past as I walk back up the street, and I see the surfboard car and the hit car driving by in the opposite direction. When I go inside the building, someone hands me another bouquet. We filmed the shot inside the lobby, when the doorman hands me the flowers, several months ago on a soundstage, and the apartment upstairs is actually a house in Orange County. We run through the scene again, with the cameras behind me this time.

Berry, the AD, wraps the shot. I find Makeup with her chair and toolbox beneath a store awning. I sit down and she starts to create a patch of road rash on my deltoid. A woman kneels on the road in front of me with a pile of loose roses, ripping off petals and stuffing them inside the tissue of a wrapped bouquet. I watch the stunt co-ordinator, Animal, cutting off the wing mirror on the driver's side with a mechanical saw and reattaching it with putty. The crew is installing a windshield you can tell is made from candy glass by the way it's a little wavy.

The film we're making is the cinematic equivalent of two-in-one shampoo and conditioner: half romcom, half action thriller. I play an FBI agent from LA who goes undercover in Miami, to date a member of a Greco-Cuban Mafia syndicate. My character's undercover as a bimbo and goes around practically bare-assed all the time, so DC can't pad up for the stunt.

She stands on the sidewalk clutching the roses and managing to look expensive in the tube dress, four-inch heels and bicep bangle. She's wearing a glassy blond wig that's meant to look like my hair, and her eyes have been made up to appear wider set. On the monitor by Theo's head, I can see a tight angle on the car. Animal climbs in and backs it out of the frame. He keeps the motor running.

BERRY
Picture's up. Quiet, please.
(*beat*)

Roll sound.

PRODUCTION SOUND MIXER

(*turns on audio*)

Sound speed.

BERRY

Roll camera.

CAMERA OPERATOR

Speed!

CLAPPER

Marker.

(*slams clapperboard*)

THEO

Action!

Animal revs the engine and swerves the car onto the sidewalk. DC tosses the bouquet and dives onto the hood. When the car brakes, she bodyslams the windscreen and it cracks. She does a back spring onto the roof of the car and falls down the side, knocking off the wing mirror and rolling towards the edge of the road. It seemed to happen too fast. Berry calls it, and DC stays down as they photograph and chalk her position.

She gets up looking like she's been rode hard and put away wet. Her lipstick's smeared and there's blood running down her arm. She walks over to the first aid station. A runner picks up the flowers and the camera crew starts to set up a shot from inside the car as the windshield is being replaced. The medic cleans the wound and sprays it with something. DC giggles and squirms.

POV (DRIVER)

Animal starts the car and puts his hands on the wheel, but keeps his foot on the brake. DC runs towards it like a gymnast approaching a vault. She flings the bouquet and flips onto the hood. She rolls towards the camera and smashes into the screen, flying up and out of the shot. The camera refocuses on the red petals in the foreground, scattered across the glass.

EXT. STREET. DAY.

I walk over to her, my heels wobbling on the uneven road surface. She's taken hers off, and is stretching her muscles.

ALEXA

That was amazing.

DC

It's a pretty basic gag. So long as you hit the car before it hits you, you can control everything that happens after that.

ALEXA

I'll be sure to give it a whirl sometime.

DC

(with a smile that says she doesn't think so)
Hey, you might just have it in you.

She does deep lunges, huffing out bursts of air. I notice she's one of those people who look less pretty with makeup, not that anyone looks good in film makeup. Her type of beauty is a kind of incandescence, and the heavy base seems to block it. I wonder if she would go out with me. We're putting in fourteen-hour days here, but maybe I could take her number and call her when we're back in LA. There are pieces of gravel stuck to her knees, and the cut on her arm has started to bleed through the concealer. I like her throwing my punches and taking my falls, as if she's protecting me.

ALEXA

Have you ever hurt yourself really badly?

DC

I broke six teeth. See?
   (*she grins and runs her fingers across them*)
These are all caps. It happened on a really easy fall. I
landed wrong, and my knee went in my mouth.

ALEXA

Ouch.

BERRY

DC, you're wrapped.

DC
   (*breezily*)
Guess I'll be seeing you.

ALEXA

Um, yah.

DC picks up her shoes and walks away.

BERRY

Alexa to the set, please.

I cross the street and lie down on the chalk marks.

DISSOLVE TO:
INT. GYM. DAWN.

DC does chest presses on a weight machine, a pale sunrise
visible in the window, streetlights still burning. She does fly
lifts with dumbbells. She tapes her hands, and punches a bag.
She doesn't pummel it, but smacks the sides, as if it's a person. She does a run-up and a crazy back flip onto a foam pad,

landing flat on her back. She does it again and again, with a different twist each time. She does push-ups on the tips of her toes with her arms stretched above her head.

INT. HOTEL ROOM. DAWN.

I'm in the shower with sudsy hair, brushing my teeth and shaving a leg at the same time. I take some meds and cup my hand under the faucet for a gulp of water to wash them down. My fingers wipe steam off a mirror to reveal my face reflected. I zip my jeans with a lit cigarette between my fingers.

EXT. NARROW ALLEY. MORNING.

DC drives a Peugeot 307 onto a half-pipe so that it flips onto its side, barely fitting in the space between two walls. She drives along the wall as if the car is skidding, and emerges on the other side. The camera crew comes around to film a close-up of one of the wheels spinning.

INT. KITCHEN. MORNING.

Mateo and I are on the kitchen island surrounded by people and lights, pretending to fuck. It's nine o'clock in the morning and my feet are hooked around his neck. After this, they'll close the set to do my nude shots. I haven't eaten a carb in seven weeks. Doing my own close-ups is kind of my thing, but I'm not sure how much longer before they'll start trying to talk me into using a body double.

EXT. SIX-LANE FREEWAY. AFTERNOON.

DC slips an earpiece into her ear and uses duct tape to secure it. She puts in her bite guard and slips on a helmet, pulls down the shatterproof visor. She slides into a yellow Leblanc Caroline that's been fitted with a roll cage. The hatch doors are pushed down, a word transmitted to her earpiece, and she steers the car onto the road. She weaves through stunt traffic, pursued by a silver Bugatti. On cue, she drives in a straight line and braces her body for impact. An eighteen-wheeler truck rear-ends the silver car, shotgunning it into the back of DC's car. She drifts the yellow car across four lanes, the tires smoking, and twirls to a stop.

INT. SCREENING ROOM. NIGHT.

Two speedboats race side-by-side on the screen, bumping against one another. A car zigzags down a wide concrete staircase teeming with pedestrians. Each time the car lunges towards a new section of the crowd, the people scatter. I smile. I scan the room, looking for her. She appears onscreen, waterskiing. She dives from a rooftop into a swimming pool. She tumbles down a flight of stairs and she does it again, ejecting a pink-puffed mule at the same point in the somersault, keeping her face hidden.

INT. HOTEL LOBBY. NIGHT.

I walk through the sliding doors, a studded night sky visible behind me. I linger by the concierge desk, touching the brochures. I step onto the elevator and hold the doors open for a while.

DISSOLVE TO:

INT. STAR ISLAND MANSION – LOUNGE. NIGHT.

The house is almost entirely made of glass, but it's brighter inside than out, so you can't see the view. I'm standing next to an outsize fishbowl that glows like a blue lantern. Bassy dance music masks the hum of low-grade anxiety, and everyone's talking at the same time, even people who are talking to each other. I can't stand these industry fuckfests, but I'm hoping I'll run into her. The stunt crew's been filming at a second location all week.

I look at the swirling confetti of tropical fish, seeing my reflection in the curve of the bowl. I applied my makeup in the speedboat and my forehead's broken out from filming in the sun every day. I'm wearing shorts because nobody told me it was black tie. People are still appearing. They arrive in pairs, as if this is Noah's Ark. It's a predominantly civilian crowd, but this is Miami, where half the population are models, and the other half are extremely good-looking. I go outside to try and bum a smoke off someone.

EXT. DECK. NIGHT.

Pop music bubbles from the speaker stacks and people flock to the standing torches like bees to honeycomb. It's a hot, sticky night so it isn't warmth they crave, but light. Exposure. The swimming pool is smooth as glass. DC's standing at the edge in a beaded green dress, frowning at the tiny candles balanced on the water. She has a bedhead, and her legs and feet are bare. I walk over to her.

                              DC
        If it isn't my acting double.

We air kiss. In her bare feet, she's the same height as me in
my heels. She appears delicate in the refracted pool light.
The normal yellow rubber band around her wrist looks like
jewelry.

                            ALEXA
        How are you enjoying Miami?

                              DC
        Yeah. It's great.
                            ALEXA
        You miss LA at all? Or someone back in LA?
                              DC
        I don't miss anything, ever.
                            ALEXA
        Seems like a useful skill to have.
                              DC
        Could be. I could probably time travel.
                            ALEXA
        Where would you go?
                              DC
                           (smiles)
        The future. That's the place for me.

I smile back. A waiter comes over and dips a tray of mimosas
at us.

                              DC
        Do you think I could get a Coke?

                          ALEXA

Scotch. Thanks.

                          WAITER

Ice?

I shake my head. DC sits on the edge of the pool and dangles
her feet in the water. I take off my shoes and do the same. The
water's warm on top and cool underneath. Its taut surface rip-
ples around our ankles and near the filter valve.

                          DC

Um, so, have you always lived in LA?

                          ALEXA

Yeah. You?

                          DC

I grew up in the Valley.

                          (*beat*)

How did you get into acting?

                          ALEXA

I was working after school as a waitress when a cast-
ing director invited me to audition for a Yoplait commercial.

                          DC

Yoplait, huh?

She looks at the sky and paddles her feet. The water splashes.

                          ALEXA

My parents wouldn't let me go. They thought he was
just some creepy guy. They're the type of immigrants
who are scared of everything.

DC

Oh? Where are they from?

ALEXA

East Germany. The old East Germany. When it was
a Socialist state.

DC

Wasn't it really hard to get out in those days?

ALEXA

They were kicked out. My father's a journalist. He
was openly critical of the regime, but they couldn't
deal with him in the usual ways because he was a
correspondent for the American press. My parents'
citizenships were revoked and they were given a day
to leave the country. They didn't return for sixteen
years. When the Wall came down, we didn't have the
money to travel there right away.

DC

Wow. I've always thought of you as this all-Ameri-
can—

ALEXA

It's very American to be a refugee.

DC

Well yeah, I just meant.

The waiter appears with our drinks. DC takes the bottle of
cola and leaves the glass on the tray. There's ice in my drink.
I wait for him to leave before I fish it out and throw it in the
pool.

ALEXA

You know in our movie, when the Mafia guys want
to kill someone, they say they're going to erase their

map? Whenever I hear that I think of my parents. They never talk about the past.

DC

Not at all?

ALEXA

I didn't even know we were German. I guess they were paranoid because the Cold War was still on. I could tell we were different, and grown-ups always asked me questions I didn't know how to answer. My father finally told me when I was ten. He said not to tell people they had lived in a Soviet state. I thought my parents were spies. Anyways. What's your family like?

DC

My mom's people are Minnesota Swedes, and my dad's side is Scotch-Irish and Russian.

ALEXA

What do they do?

DC

We're a stunt family. My great-grandfather was an ex-convict who got paid by a studio to jump off a house into a wagon full of hay, and managed to hustle it into a regular gig. He ended up buying a ranch and turning it into a stunt school, which my uncle and aunt run now. You know Animal's my dad, right? You've probably worked with my cousins, too.

ALEXA

No way—you're Animal's kid?

DC

You know, I even met you before? He took me on the set of one of your movies, and I begged him to introduce us. At the time, I wanted to be an actress.

                    ALEXA
Weird, I don't remember. I know I met your broth-
ers when they were teenagers. They were gorgeous.
Golden.

                      DC
That was me! And my older brother.

                    ALEXA
                (*a finger to the lips*)
Sorry. My memory's shot.

                      DC
No, you're right. I was a boy then.

She looks at me in a hopeful way. I wait for the hidden face to
reveal itself, for her to split into two, the way people do when
they tell you they used to be someone else. She just looks the
same.

                      DC
I—don't usually lay that on people right away. I just
couldn't believe you remembered me.

                    ALEXA
You had skateboards. You showed me some tricks.

                      DC
                   (*laughs*)
You were really nice to us. We both had mad crushes
on you after that.

She sets her bottle down, the glass making a low tone against
the flagstone.

                    ALEXA
Thank you for telling me.

DC

You must get that a lot, people spilling their guts because they feel like they know you.

ALEXA

I don't mind. I get tongue-tied around strangers, so usually I'm just glad one of us is talking.

DC

I always thought it was cool that you were out, you know, to the public. It made me feel like there was going to be room in the world for me, too.

ALEXA

It wasn't a conscious decision. Everything happened so fast, it just never occurred to me to lie. But I'd do it the same way again.

DC

In this business, you can't escape yourself. There's always someone who remembers you.

She smiles with one side of her mouth. A woman's obnoxious laughter peals across the deck. Theo and Berry are standing under one of the torches, trying to raise the extra four million dollars from the guy who owns this house. He looks like he's still in high school. If they see me, they'll want me to go over and say hi.

ALEXA

Feel like getting out of here?

DC

Definitely.

We pull our legs out of the water and I try to dry my feet on the flagstone. I step into my shoes and follow her dark, wet prints across the deck. As she walks she sweeps her hair up on top of her head and palms the gleam off the back of her neck. She lets the hair fall.

EXT. OPEN-TOP SPEEDBOAT – BISCAYNE BAY. NIGHT.

The outboard motor roars. Salt spray mists our faces as the boat chops across the glossy black waves. The lights in the bay glitter like earrings on a carpet, and a closed-top boat shaped like spacecraft overtakes us, pushing a V through the water.

ALEXA
(*shouting*)
I mean, you're welcome to come hang out.

Her mouth moves, the wind eating her words. She smiles and looks away. I breathe the ocean's tinny scent and look at her hand next to mine on the seat. She has thin fingers and small shiny nails. I want to slip my hand on top of hers, but I don't remember how to touch people. It's been a while.

FLASHBACK TO:
LOS ANGELES, THREE YEARS AGO

The last person I dated was my dog walker. She's smart to the point of being borderline insane, but is funny and knows how to cook. She was writing a spec script about Chinese immigrants working on the Pacific Railroad. To this day, I know more than I've ever cared to about the intricacies of carving a rail bed through the Sierra Nevadas. I sat through hours of moldy documentary footage and trudged through ill-lit museums in several states and Canadian provinces.

When the script was ready I threw my weight around a little, and *Celestials* sold outright, to a major. I took her out to celebrate, and she dumped me before I sank my teeth into the appetizer.

I went on a talk show without taking my hay fever pill, and when the host asked me about her, my eyes looked shimmery. Since then I've been the poster child for bummed-out single people. I was glad when *Celestials* got stuck in development hell for a year before getting axed.

INT. HOTEL HALLWAY. NIGHT.

She follows me down the corridor, carrying her shoes. I slide my key-card and the lights flash green. I can see my call sheet sticking out from under the door.

INT. HOTEL ROOM. NIGHT

The room is warm and stuffy. I check my call time for tomorrow, toss the sheet in the trash, and turn down the thermostat. The air-conditioning comes on. It makes a swishing sound. We take off our shoes.

> ALEXA

Want some wine?

> DC

I don't mind.

> ALEXA
> (*looks for corkscrew*)

You can move those clothes off the chair.

> DC

Come here.

I turn around. She's sitting right behind me on the edge of the bed. I push her down and climb on top of her. She's a soft kisser, hiding her teeth. Her mouth tastes cold and sweet, and I can smell her sunscreen. I put my hands in her hair and kiss her more. She starts grinding against me. I stand up and take off my top. As I take off my shorts, I watch her kneel on the bed and pull her dress up over her head. I see white cotton underpants, a tanned stomach with a tear-shaped navel, and high tits with perfectly centered nipples. My clit's so hard it hurts. I stand at the foot of the bed and take off my bra. I push up my breasts and start licking one of my nipples, watching her face change. When she reaches for it, I nudge her hand away and keep doing it. She reaches into her underwear and starts touching herself. She does it slowly at first, then she grits her teeth and rubs so hard that her breasts shake. Her eyes are as strong and dark as blood. She comes hard and recovers fast.

She pulls me onto the bed and starts sucking my tits. She makes soft sounds as she does it. My cunt's throbbing. When she tries to touch it, I push her hand away and shove her into the pillows. I bite and lick her thighs and stomach. They're covered with the tiniest blond hairs. I twirl her nipples until the tips stick up. I keep twirling them. She clutches the sheets and moves her hips. I stroke the cleft of her cunt through her underpants. Her lips feel puffy and warm through the cotton. I run my finger along the join of her thigh. It's slick with come. I reach in through the leg elastic and slide two fingers inside her. She works her hips as I move them slowly in and out. She's slippery and tight. I push them up to the knuckle and press her clit with my thumb. She makes sounds. I pull her underpants down over her legs. I spread her lips and lick her out, my nipples rubbing against the sheet until I come. I moan with my mouth on her and she starts coming too.

I pin down her thighs and keep licking and sucking. She keeps coming. Each time I swallow, she floods my mouth. Flicking her clit with my tongue, I start to fuck her with two fingers, fast and hard enough to make her tits bounce. When I add my thumb and slow it down, she starts to moan and talk and touch them. I stop licking and fingerfuck her for a while, so I can watch. I switch to four fingers, no thumb, speeding up and slowing down. When I put my thumb in her asshole she comes, and when I pull it out she comes again. I spread her apart and start eating her out. When I look up, I see sloping stomach and the peachy undersides of her tits. I reach up and touch them. I suck and bite her clit, pinching and twisting the tips of her nipples. She bucks and screams, filling my mouth.

DISSOLVE TO:

POV (CEILING)

The air-conditioning cools our skin. She turns her head, a lock of hair falling across her eyes. I tuck it behind her ear.

ALEXA

You seeing anyone?

DC

Dating isn't really a big thing for me. I think I develop more through my friendships.

ALEXA
(beat)

Oh.

DC

Aren't you going to ask me anything? People always ask me all these things.

ALEXA

You must be sick of answering stupid questions.

DC

You won't ask anything stupid.

ALEXA

Have you always known?

DC

I mean, I knew that how I felt in the world was different from how I was supposed to feel. I was more talkative than most boys and I liked the way that women and girls talked to each other, but I also liked cars and sports and fishing. In some ways it was more confusing because I wasn't alienated from my masculinity. Until I was fifteen, I understood only that it had something to do with the way I wanted to be treated. I sensed my life was going to be a bit less—automatic than it is for other people.

ALEXA

How did you figure it out?

DC

I used to stay at the stunt ranch in the summers. There was nothing to do at my house. At the ranch I could train and there were car ramps and half-pipes for me to skate on. I had a crush on one of my girl cousins. The summer she got her driver's license, she was never home. I snuck into her room one afternoon.

There was a light blue Polo shirt-dress lying on the floor, and I picked it up and stuck my nose in it. Breathing in the smell of perfume and cotton and girl sweat, I felt this rush of really strong energy. It was like the feeling you got when you were a kid and you uncovered some mystery of the adult world, and you knew you'd discovered something you shouldn't have, but you didn't know exactly what it was. That mixture of excitement and power and fear.

I took the dress to my room and locked the door. I didn't know what I wanted to do with it. I laid it on the bed and looked at it for a while before deciding to put it on. As the material slipped over my body, I began to feel lit up. I looked in the mirror and something switched on—a sense of rightness, but so distant, it felt like sadness.

ALEXA

(*breathless*)

That's beautiful.

DC

(*smiles*)

Let's do this again sometime.

ALEXA

I'd like that. I get back from rushes around midnight or one, usually.

She pulls the blanket up to her ear. I turn off the light and listen to her breathing getting slower and deeper. I think about all the things she's told me tonight. I picture the great-grandfather jumping into a hay wagon, and a teenage boy in a T-shirt dress, looking into a mirror and seeing a new life.

DISSOLVE TO:

INT. STAR ISLAND MANSION – MASTER BEDROOM. DAY.

Makeup cuts a hole in my top and starts making a bullet entry wound on my chest. She builds a crater out of eyelash glue and cotton wool, before painting the hole black. While the paint dries, she puts the finishing touches on the exit wound on my back. The other girl did my normal makeup before starting on the cuts and scrapes. Right now she's making a deep gash on my thigh.

Makeup comes back around to the front of me and applies concealer onto the cotton wool. She uses a paintbrush to stipple rust-red paint on top and blends it a bit with her finger. She pinches all around the crater to make the ridge sharper, and daubs fake blood over the black-painted hole until it forms a rivulet. A drop lands on my arm. I lick it off. It tastes like icing. It's made of food coloring and liquid glucose. When I filmed out in Hong Kong, their fake blood tasted like cough syrup. Makeup says she'll add some more right before we shoot.

CAMERA MOVES WITH HER

I put on my shoes and go out into the hall, catching a glimpse of my bloody reflection in the mirror by the door. I take out my ponytail and push the hair band onto my wrist, passing Theo on the stairs. He's eating yoghurt from a tub and talking on a headset. I point to an imaginary watch and mime smoking a cigarette. He nods, and I go downstairs.

When I reach the foyer, a woman walks out of the kitchen in a T-shirt that says MEDIC. She does a double take when she sees me, and then she laughs. I cut through the living room, where crew are setting up cameras and lights, and sliding a breakaway wall in front of the real wall. Someone is taping small explosive devices to the back of a painting. Two men push a tall display cabinet against the fake wall. They start unpacking glassware from a box, dropping squibs into the glasses and vases before placing them in the cabinet.

EXT. DECK. DAY.

Wardrobe walks up to me and checks the Polaroid in her hand before taking the band off my wrist. She runs her finger along the indentation on my skin and tells me to rub it to make it spring back faster. I mooch a cigarette from her. DC is sitting at the picnic table with her father. They're busy planning something with Matchbox cars, so I don't go over. I didn't know Animal had a prosthetic leg until a few years ago, when I saw it fly off in a stunt explosion. Someone told me he'd had a car accident on the way to work.

As they head inside, DC sees me and waves, pulling a face to acknowledge my gruesome makeup. It's late afternoon and the sun has dropped behind the clouds. I go over and sit at the table and roll one of the toy cars back and forth. The glass wall of the house reflects me with the pool and the ocean behind me. When the lights come on inside, the reflection disappears.

INT. LIVING ROOM (THROUGH GLASS). DAY.

The painting with the squibs has been mounted on the fake wall. DC runs across the set, brandishing a Glock 23. Mateo's stunt double chases her, firing blanks, and a trail of tiny explosions tears across the painting and the wall. The glass panes of the cabinet dissolve, and the vases, snifters and flutes burst one by one. The lights go out, and the window turns into a mirror again.

INT. LIVING ROOM. DAY.

I come in through the side doors, almost tripping over a sheet of glass propped against the wall. Some of the crew are over at the far end of the room, striking the set, while others prepare a new set-up at this end. I watch a man carefully dusting the surface of a wooden coffee table with powder. He places a penny at each corner of the table, and tops each penny with a screw. He comes over and glues a squib to the centre of the glass pane before picking it up and lowering it onto the table so it rests on the screws.

DC's standing by the piano in a black bra that shows the tops of her tits, sticking a plate to her chest with medical tape. She tapes a squib to the centre of the plate, puts her top back on, and tapes a blood bag on top of her clothes, over the squib. She picks up a pouch of blood and hides it in her hand. Make-up makes me stand on a raincoat while she uses a pipette to drizzle blood on my clothes.

They get everything running, and Theo calls action. Animal counts backwards from five and presses a switch on a remote. The squib on DC's chest detonates as she leaps backwards, and the blood bag bursts, unleashing a dark, syrupy scribble. The charge on the coffee table explodes and the glass breaks just before she lands, the table bursting apart like a diagram. The candy glass makes a spattering sound instead of tinkling. She writhes on the glass, clutching the pouch of blood to her heart and pumping it so the color pulses through her fingers onto the floor. Berry calls a cut and wrap. DC stands up with her hand over one eye and walks off into the foyer. I want to find out if she's okay, but Hair is brushing my hair and spraying it. Berry calls for me again. I walk onto the set, stepping over the glass slivers.

INT. HOTEL HALLWAY. NIGHT.

I knock. I hear sounds inside the room. DC opens the door, gauze taped over one eye.

ALEXA

Jesus. Are you okay?

DC

Yeah I'm good. Come in.

She's wrapped in a blue silk robe embroidered with gold butterflies. It opens a little when she holds the door and I want to touch her, but I brush past.

INT. HOTEL ROOM. NIGHT.

Canned laughter jangles on the TV set. There's an open suitcase on the bed, filled with books and stretchy workout cords. I put my bag on the chair.

DC

(*picks up remote, kills the sound*)

I went up to see you earlier.

ALEXA

What happened?

DC

I got some stunt glass in my eye. When I take a fall, I have to keep them open to see where I'm going, and I didn't get them closed them in time. I think I was tired.

ALEXA

Oh no.

DC

They've called out another double. She's not a driver, but the guys'll cover.

ALEXA

Will you be okay?

                    DC

I need surgery. I have to do it in LA, it's something
with my insurance. I'm catching the red-eye tonight.

                  ALEXA

I should let you get back to it.

                    DC

Call me.

I nod. She smiles. I pick up my bag and walk to the door.

DISSOLVE TO:
DOWNTOWN LOS ANGELES, TWO WEEKS LATER
EXT. RESTAURANT PATIO. NIGHT.

It's warm and breezy, and the clinking of cutlery punctuates
the smooth jazz oozing from the speakers. DC strides across
the terrace, looking tanned and healthy in a tiny sundress and
flip-flops, and carrying a balled-up sweater. I stand up and
hug her, smelling the sun and wind in her hair. The candle-
light plays on her face as she drapes her sweater over the back
of her chair and sits down. Her eye looks fine, a little blood-
shot. She opens the menu and scans the pages quickly before
closing it again.

                  ALEXA

How are you?

                    DC

I'm good. I'm great.

                  WAITER

Would you like to hear about the specials?

DC

I'll have the steak. Blue, please.

ALEXA

And a Cobb salad for me. Can I have the dressing on the side?

WAITER
(*takes the menus*)

To drink?

ALEXA

Coffee, black, no sugar.

DC

Water's fine.

ALEXA

So.

DC

Yeah. What've you been up to?

ALEXA

As little as possible, really. I only have another week off. I've been swimming every morning and then vegging out for the rest of the day.

DC

What are you doing next?

ALEXA

Playing Levi Geffen's mother in the new Gabor Benedek project.

DC

Levi? He's not that much younger than you.

ALEXA

I know, right? It's insulting. Still, this is the first lesbian character I've been offered who isn't damaged beyond belief.

The waiter brings my coffee. I take a sip.

> ALEXA

I'm shooting that for six months, and then I'm heading out to Germany to work with this kid, Sommer Zweig. Young writer-director, fresh out of film school. My cousin was her teacher, and she passed along a script. It was waiting for me when I came back from Miami. Normally I don't read every random thing people send me, but I'd been thinking I wanted to try something new. I just loved it.

> DC

So you're in touch with your family out there?

> ALEXA

Not really, no. Not at all. My parents are, but—that's kind of a neat thing that's happening because of it.

> DC

That's great.

> ALEXA
> (*shyly*)

Yeah, so. You back at work yet?

> DC

I'm not going back.

> ALEXA
> (*beat*)

Are you serious?

> DC

The surgery didn't take. I can't see out of this eye at all anymore.

> (*touches her cheek*)

> ALEXA

Fuck. I had no idea it was so bad.

DC

Me neither. At least, I figured on being lucky.

ALEXA

But why do you have to give up stunts? You can still
see fine, right?

DC

I have no depth perception. Everything just looks flat.
Doing stunts is about matching time against space. I
can't do that anymore. I was fully insured, so.

(*sips water*)

I'm thinking about getting out.

ALEXA

You mean, leaving LA?

DC

When it sank in that I'll have to start over, I thought:
why not make it exactly how I want it to be?

ALEXA

How do you mean?

DC

As a woman. Where nobody knows.

Our food arrives. DC tucks her napkin into the neckline of
her dress and starts dismantling her steak. I drizzle half the
dressing over my salad. We chew our food, the restaurant
noise and color swirling around us. Every time our eyes meet,
she looks like she's about to say something, but flattens her
mouth into a line instead.

ALEXA

(*puts down fork, pushes plate away*)

Seems like a big decision to be making when you've
just been through so much.

                              DC

It's not the first time I've thought about it. I just never
imagined it would be possible because of work, you
know, and my family's industry connections.

                            ALEXA

What's your plan?

                              DC

To leave as soon as I can. I don't want to be here. I
miss doing stunts, and all anyone ever talks about in
this town is movies.

                            ALEXA

I wish you wouldn't disappear before we find out
how our thing plays out. Or maybe this *is* our thing
playing out.

                              DC

No, not at all. I'd be into it if I wasn't leaving, it's
just—I need this more.

                            ALEXA

Maybe we don't have to call it off. Once you get settled, I'll come over, and we'll see where we are.

                              DC

I like you a lot. I wish we could do this. The thing is,
I'm going deep stealth. That means wiping the slate
clean.

                            ALEXA
                 (*gulps coffee, pulls a face*)
Ugh. It's cold. How clean are we talking? Like, what
about your family?

DC bites her lip and shakes her head.

> ALEXA
> *(softly)*

Really?

> DC

I'll never come back to LA.

> ALEXA

Does it have to be like that?

> DC

Everyone I know has known me since I was—a kid. It's very limiting.

> ALEXA

Yeah, okay. I get that.

> *(coldly)*

Are you done?

> *(gestures to waiter for bill)*

> DC

So listen, do you need to take off, or? You want to come over?

> ALEXA

I—that sounds nice.

> DC

You driving?

> ALEXA
> *(relaxing a little)*

I'm on a bike.

> DC

Perfect. We'll strap it to the ski rack.

> ALEXA

I wish I hadn't met you until after. On the other side. But then, I don't know where we would've met. Maybe in a store or something.

                    DC
                 (*smiling*)
Yeah.

                  (*sadly*)
Maybe.

INT. CAR. NIGHT.
REAR PROJECTION (STREETS OF L.A.)

The sky is the spooky, bright color of blue screen. DC pilots the car with jaunty precision. The motion of the car feels unusually smooth, and at the same time I can feel each squeak and nudge, every nuance in the contact between rubber and road. I watch the blocks of light and shadow intercutting on her face.

                  ALEXA
Don't I make you feel good? You know what I see when I look at you, right?
                    DC
          (*keeping her eyes on the road*)
There's no point doing this unless I do it perfect. I'm sorry. I don't know what else to say.

She indicates before switching lanes.

INT. LIVING ROOM. NIGHT.

DC flicks on a light and disappears into the kitchen. The apartment smells like a clean T-shirt. It has a glossy wood floor and an unusually high ratio of lamps to furniture. I hear the suck of the fridge door, and beer tops popping. She comes out and hands me one.

INT. BEDROOM. NIGHT.

She shuts the door. We sit on the edge of the bed, sipping our beers. The sheets gleam in the light from the building opposite. She takes the bottle from my hand and sets it on the floor and pulls me down on the bed. We make out, taking off each other's clothes.

> ALEXA
> I'm too sad to be a decent lay right now. I don't want our last time to be depresso sex.

DC sighs and flops onto her back. I get under the sheet. We're quiet for a while.

POV (CEILING)

> ALEXA
> Where will you go?

> DC
> I don't know. A small, stuffy town in the Midwest. Or Vermont, or Maine.

> ALEXA
> Why stuffy? Isn't it better to go somewhere liberal, or a big city where you can disappear?

> DC
> The narrower people are, the farther it'll be from their minds.

> ALEXA
> Oh.
> (beat)
> What will you do there?

DC

I'll be a receptionist or—something low-key and girly, anyway. The insurance payout was big enough that I don't need to work again ever, but people will scrutinize me if I don't appear to have a job. I need a new story, but I haven't been able to think of anything boring enough. The goal is to make people fall asleep the minute I start talking about my life.

ALEXA

How will you explain why people can't meet your family or any of your old friends?

DC

I don't know, exactly. I haven't had enough time to think it all through.

ALEXA

You could say you're divorced, and all your friends sided with your ex. It happens.

DC

Mm, yeah. That way I'll get a grace period before people start trying to set me up. I don't want to get involved with anyone until I've existed for a while. I should accumulate at least a year of history first. How about my parents? I don't want to say they're dead, it seems kind of—

ALEXA

They live in another country and they don't like to fly. You always go out there to visit them.

DC

You're really good at this.

ALEXA

But how are you going to meet other lesbians if you live in such a conservative place?

DC

I'm not. The whole idea is to fly beneath the radar.

ALEXA

Uh—I don't get it.

DC

I'm going all the way with this. I'll stick a flag in my lawn and go to church every Sunday, and marry a man. I'll be part of the superstructure.

ALEXA

Wow.

DC

This is going to unlock a whole new level.

ALEXA

It's just—I thought this was about being who you really are. You like women.

DC

If I wanted to be an outsider all my life, I'd just stay here.

ALEXA

Oh my God. Can you hear yourself?

DC

I want the life I want. I don't care how it plays to anyone else. I'm not auditioning for *The Vagina Monologues*.

ALEXA

(*laughs*)

Okay. Okay. And if you're not happy, or you don't like it, you'll come back?

DC

I can't think like that and anyway, I don't know what I'll have left to come back for. It's like you're saying to people, I'm perfectly fine with never seeing you again. My friends—some of those relationships are already over.

> ALEXA

Have you told your family?

> DC

Oh God, they went crazy. And I feel bad, I mean. They've always been so cool about me. My dad was all, it's not like you're being *persecuted*. Everyone accepts you, isn't that enough? I don't know. Maybe it should be.

She gets under the sheet and lets me hold her. I stroke her back. It's warm and silky.

> ALEXA

Will you love him?

> DC

Who? Oh. I'll try. I want to be in it for the long haul, and I think things last longer if you just really *like* the person. I don't know how useful love is, in the long run.

> (*yawns*)

> ALEXA

> (*hugging her*)

I hope you make it, DC. I hope when you get there, it's great, and you're happy. I do.

DC EVAPORATES IN MATCH CUT TO:
POTSDAM, SIX MONTHS LATER
INT. HOTEL ROOM. NIGHT.

Snow falls outside my window. I'm watching rolling news

with the sound down, mesmerized by the ticker-tape trawling across the bottom of the screen. I'm here for five months shooting on a sound stage at Studio Babelsberg for *Tell Them*, a left-field production based on the kidnapping of Patty Hearst and the choreography of Pina Bausch. The dance numbers are set not to music but to Patty's stoned, sibilant drawl on the audiotapes, her lockjawed accent virtually dripping money.

We're shooting against green screen, to be chroma keyed with a grainy, washed-out San Francisco. Another team is out there now, filming backgrounds with a Fisher-Price Pixel-Vision. I've seen footage, and it's breathtaking. I'm glad I decided to work with Sommer. She's really going for something. I play Mrs Catherine Hearst in bouffant hairdo and twin pearls. I'm working for next-to-nothing, which in itself is kind of liberating, and I'm getting free German lessons and dance training. And I have my own reasons for being here.

My cellphone rings. I sit up and find it on the nightstand. There's something weird with my service provider and US numbers aren't showing up, even if they're on my contact list. It's just after dinnertime in California, so it's probably my mother. If I answer this late, she'll want to know why I'm not asleep. I let it go to voicemail.

My Aunt Elfi and Uncle Walter live an hour away, in Leipzig. We came to stay with them the summer I was fifteen, two years after the Wall came down. I had never heard my parents speak German before. My cool-eyed cousins Franka and Lena, with their drab, shiny faces, and modelesque bodies girded in acid-washed denim, intimidated the shit out of me. I spent the whole vacation hunched in front of the TV, demolishing mountains of strange, heavy food. I've avoided coming here ever since, and have snubbed the Berlinale so many times my agent says I'm probably blacklisted.

Franka lives here in Potsdam and teaches at the film school, so we get together for drinks some nights. On weekends we drive to Leipzig to see Elfi and Walter, and sometimes Lena comes up from Berlin with her boyfriend and their three beautiful brats. Aunt Elfi is my dad's sister and was best friends with my mom, which is how my parents got together, another story they never told me. I've been finding out all kinds of things. My grandfather died in Sachsenhausen after the war, when it was a Soviet-run Silence camp. And my father had been a Young Pioneer who pledged allegiance to Stalin, and chased Colorado beetles.

My mother grew up in Leipzig, too, but she's an only child and her mom and grandparents died before she ever made it back. Elfi said my mother's stepdad left when the border was opened. He didn't say where he was headed, and he probably didn't know. My phone's flashing. I decide to call my voicemail.

AUTOMATED VOICE OVER

To listen to your messages, press 1. To manage your greetings—

I press 1.

You have one new message. First new message. Received today at four-twelve.

DC (V.O.)

Alexa, hi. It's me.

(*pause*)

I don't know why I'm calling, I just. Hi.

ALEXA

(*softly*)

Hi.

> DC
> (*laughs*)

It's so stupid, I keep waiting for you to answer. Ahm, so I'm okay, I'm really good and I—you know, last night I dreamed I was doing a gag? I jumped through a window, but the glass wasn't candy glass.

> (*beat*)

I felt it. I can even eat something in a dream and be able to taste it.

> (*pause*)

I shouldn't be doing this.

> ALEXA

I won't tell.

> DC

I think about you sometimes.

> ALEXA

Where are you?

> AUTOMATED (V.O.)

End of messages. To listen to this message again, press 2. To save this message, press 3. To delete—

I press 2.

DISSOLVE TO:

EXT. GRAUMAN'S CHINESE THEATRE. FALL. NIGHT.

Camera bulbs are popping behind the hazy glare of the cine lights. I smile with Vaselined teeth and stare into the glitter storm, turning my head and focusing beyond the pulses of light to keep from blinking. It's drizzling. I realize I'm shivering. The flashguns make a clipping sound, like garden shears.

PHOTOGRAPHERS

Alexa!   Alexa! Over here!

Alexa, right here, please!

To your left, please, to your left!

And straight ahead please!

One more over here!

Hey, beautiful!

Good girl!   Looking this way!

One more time!

The theatre's pagoda-style centerpiece towers behind me, a bas-relief dragon twisted on its face, Ming dogs guarding its red columns. The film's title is spelled across the courtyard in letters chiseled from blocks of ice, and I'm standing in front of the A, grinning and trying to relax my neck muscles, and worrying that the lamé dress looks too stripper. My cheek starts twitching. I can't feel the shape of my smile, and I'm concerned it may have turned into a snarl. I try to think friendly thoughts as I put my hands on my waist and change my leg position. I tilt my head forward so the rain will catch in my hair instead of wrecking my makeup. At this angle, twinkly eyes can look a bit menacing, so I narrow them slightly and make my gaze softer as I continue to sweep it back and forth.

I switch up the eyebrows, so it's more like, *hey, isn't this great?* I do the helpless modesty laugh, pushing my shoulders forward and collapsing inward slightly. A seven-foot bouncer steps into my field of vision and makes a hand signal. I wave to the photographers and move towards the crush of fans spilling over the metal barricade.

People call my name. I touch their outstretched palms. This is my favorite part. I like the honesty of hands. I take people's phones and snap photos of myself with them, leaning back so it looks like we're standing beside each other, but not so much that I get a double chin. I autograph an arm, an antiquated issue of *DIVA*, and several copies of a stoner flick in which I played a total space cadet fifteen years ago. I speak to someone's sister in Tennessee and pose for a few more pictures before blowing kisses and walking into the publicity swarm.

REPORTER

(*holds up the mic and speaks in a commanding, musical tone*)

I'm Palomino Tang and *F-word* is in Los Angeles tonight! We're on Hollywood Boulevard at the world premiere of this season's hottest ticket: *Criminal People*, starring Alexa Ritter and Mateo Marino. I'm here with the star of the film for an *F-word* exclusive. Hi, Alexa!

ALEXA

Hello!

REPORTER

Now the first thing *F-word* viewers will want to know is, who are you wearing?

ALEXA

1920s Dior.

REPORTER

And how about this scrumptious choker, what is it *made* of? It looks like soap bubbles, and rubies.

ALEXA

It's a custom piece by an up-and-coming local designer called Justine O. She blows these glass bubbles by mouth and fills each one with her own tears or blood.

REPORTER

How fun! Now, your character in the film is keeping a deadly secret, and I'm hoping you'll let *F-word* viewers in on *your* secrets. Do you have any secret, guilty pleasures?

ALEXA

Um—I eat whipped cream out of the can sometimes.

REPORTER

Fabulous. Excellent. Anything else our viewers will want to know about?

ALEXA

I'm starring in *Thanksgiving* with Levi Geffen and Bambi Sawyer. It opens the day after Thanksgiving.

REPORTER

Wonderful. Marvelous. Thanks so much for talking to us.

ALEXA

Oh. Thanks, *F-word*.

INT. THEATRE. NIGHT.

The house lights have gone down but one of the spots at the front is still on, projecting a moon onto the gold trees stitched on the red silk curtain covering the screen. People clap and whistle as Theo enters the spotlight, holding a huge wireless mic and a tiny acid-pink Post-it. My mouth feels dry and I wish I had a piece of gum or something, but I didn't bring a purse because I always end up losing it at these things. Mateo and his boyfriend are sitting to my left, and one of the executive producers, whose name always eludes me, is to my right. I'll look out for it in the credits so I can speak to her afterwards.

THEO

Criminal People has been almost three years in the
pipeline, and I want to extend my deepest thanks
to everyone involved. Berry, Jonno, Miles, Mateo,
Alexa, Animal, Greg, and—I've loved every minute
working with you guys.

(shrugs)

Enjoy the film.

The spot goes out. Everyone claps again, and the curtains
sashay apart. The logo intro runs, letters bashing into one
another to make other letters appear, and the screen goes
black and music starts to play. The studio name appears, then
Theo's name. We see a finger writing the film's title on fogged
glass. After a few seconds, the letters steam over. The opening credits are superimposed over a continuous shot of a car
driving along the Malibu coastline, its windows flashing in
the sun.

ALEXA (V.O.)

I think that's her. I recognize the way she handles
the car, like a body, with the right amount of reck-
lessness and greed. Last summer, I tracked down
all the movies she's been in and watched them on a
loop. I played and replayed those balletic car spins,
her countless hard falls and near misses, freezing
the picture and trying to catch a glimpse of her face.
I looked for her everywhere, in all the movies, even
the new ones. I guess I still believed she was out there
in some celluloid galaxy, crashing cars and jumping
through windows. But when I heard her voice on the
machine, I understood. She's somewhere else now.

I picture her living in a two-story duplex, sugar maples growing in a shared front yard heaped in gold light and red leaves. In her town, people leave their doors unlocked, and children walk to school. She might be working as a bank teller. She'll be dating by now. I imagine a slightly overweight divorcé with soft, fat fingers and pretty eyes, who teaches science at the high school. He has a young son and daughter who come to stay with him every other weekend, and he doesn't want to have any more children. He washes his car every Sunday, and his favorite expression is *What the hey*.

This weekend the kids will be at his ex's. DC and the science teacher will drive in his four-by-four to the nearest big town and spend the morning at Sears, picking out a tent. They're planning to go camping in the Poconos. Later they'll park outside the deli on Fourth and split a meatball sub. They'll sit at the counter by the window, reading the marquee of the two-screen cinema opposite. She'll say, *Oh*, and he'll say, *I wouldn't mind seeing that. Look, it's on in less than half an hour.* They'll cross the street and buy tickets and popcorn and soda.

At first they'll be the only ones sitting inside the theatre, playing along to the movie quiz on the screen. She'll turn to him and say, *I should have brought a sweater*, and he'll say, *I might have something in the trunk, it's kind of like a poncho*, and she'll say, *No, don't worry.* He'll put his soda in the cup holder and rub her arms. She'll hold his buttery hand in her lap, clutching it tighter during the car chases.

When the film ends, he'll stand up the second the

credits start rolling, and she'll remain seated. He'll glance at the other people leaving, and then he'll push his seat back down and sit on the very end of it. He'll watch her reading intently about who the dolly grip was, and things like that, and he'll decide he likes this about her, the way she gives things her full attention and doesn't like to rush. He'll start to feel that the other people are being greedy and disrespectful. When the house lights come on, she'll blink her eyes and smile at him in a dazed way. He'll hold her hand all the way to the car, and they'll talk about the movie on the drive home.

Ghosts

She's scraping leftovers onto a porcelain plate. "Are you bringing a bag?"

"No. Just my gym bag." I tear off a sheet of plastic film and hand it to her.

She stretches it over the pieces of wilted meat. Her nails are freshly clipped, the edges crisp and hexagonal.

"So yes," she says, smoothing down the edges of the film. "You mean yes, but you like to say no." She smiles, showing teeth. The black tiles behind her reflect the track lighting as hundreds of brilliant dots.

"What are we talking about?"

"A gym bag's a bag." She puts the plate in the fridge.

I touch my stomach under my T-shirt. "You never know, tonight might be relaxing."

"Staying here is relaxing." The fridge door's closed, but she's still holding the handle.

"Think of it as our bedroom, just halfway across town."

"Doesn't that defeat the purpose?"

"We can't put it off again. Our session's on Monday."

"I know," she says. "Do you think I don't know?"

The hotel room is pale gray with violet accents and a view that takes up an entire wall. AJ opens the closet door. She's tall and brisk in her stretchy tank dress and basketball shoes. She used to have long hair that was calm and sleepy, but she recently had it lopped into a cartoonish bob that ruffles with her movements.

"What do you expect you'll find in there?" I ask.

"I like to know how much space we have." She closes it.

"You never use it."

"I might."

She walks around, playing with the lighting. I start unpacking my bag onto the desk. Tonight is Dr Barry's idea. He's not even really a doctor. We've been going to him ever since AJ found out I'd been seeing a professional domme. The domme's name is Satine. She's been in the picture much longer than AJ. She was my first and only top. The sex was perfect but the love was bad, a Möbius strip.

AJ comes over to touch things. She finds the bubblebath I brought. "Why did you bring shampoo?"

I tell her it's bubblebath.

"You went out and bought this? For tonight?" She twists off the cap and sniffs the contents.

"Isn't that what people do?"

She puts the bottle down. "I'm just surprised."

The bottom rows of her lashes are as thick as stitches. I kiss her on the mouth. She locks in, keeps it going for a while. We open our eyes.

"Okay," I say. "Let's do this."

We switch off our phones. As the beeping subsides, I wonder which is better: to apologize for our being stuck here, or to thank her for coming.

"Maybe something good will happen," I say.

As a child, she had fallen out of a tree, cutting her face on one of its branches. The scar is still visible in certain light. It deepens when she smiles.

Music plays in the lift. I think it's the theme song of an old TV show. We watch the floor numbers lighting.

"My student halls were just around the corner from here," she says.

The lift opens. We cross the lobby and push the doors. It's a hot, clear night. The sky is embedded with cold bright chips of light.

"What do you think Dr Barry expects us to say tonight that we haven't already said?" AJ says as we head up the road.

"We have to stop calling him that. I almost said it to his face the other day."

"Do you think he knows he looks like Barry Manilow?"

"He must. I think he tries to accentuate it."

"It may be the reason I've trusted him from the beginning," she says.

I watch her hair bouncing. When she had it cut, it made me sad because I thought she might have been punishing herself with fantasies about what Satine looks like. She has meticulously avoided the subject. I think she imagines someone lush and obvious, pneumatic. Satine's in her fifties and looks like a violin teacher. I chose her specifically because I hadn't found her tight, polished face too appealing in the photos. I thought I'd be less likely to become infatuated. You'd think AJ would be pleased if she knew this, but it would probably slay her. She's very threatened by unbeautiful women who have power over men.

There are no cars on the cross streets. We walk past dimmed

shop glass and the uplit lobbies of office buildings. In one, a watchman sits on a swivel chair by the doors.

"Have you ever had a truly menial job?" AJ asks me, as we walk beneath a net of trees.

"I worked in a crisp factory. I'm sure I've told you."

"I like it when you tell me things," she says.

"I had to wear a see-through shower cap and stare at crisps going by on a conveyor belt. My job was to pick out the ones that looked too burned. I kept seeing Marc Bolan's face on the chips, stenciled in barbecue powder."

"How old were you?"

"Sixteen," I say. "What were you doing?"

"I was still at school, smoking incredibly thin roll-ups."

I smile at her. As we cross under the railway bridge, the steel track shivers with the premonition or the memory of a distant train.

"Why have I never seen marks?" she says.

It's been like this lately. I finally figured out that there's a conversation progressing in her head all the time, and every so often, she tunes me in.

"She was careful," I say. Satine wore a glove when she spanked me. She rubbed ointment on my skin to soften it before she whipped me. Most of the marks went away after a few hours. I took vitamins.

AJ cuts me a sideways glance. "Is that why you do kick-boxing?"

"What?"

"In case you ended up with a black eye? Do you even *have* kickboxing?"

"Of course."

"God." She leans forward, as if braving weather.

"I'm sorry."

"Stop saying that. I've already forgiven you."

"Let's talk about the concept of forgiveness."

"Fuck you," she says, "and fuck Dr Barry. That man is making money from our inertia."

A car zooms past, the sound underlining her words.

"I'm starting to worry it's not in my nature," she says after a while.

"To forgive?"

"Do you really think people change?"

We stop walking and look at each other. "No," I say, "they don't change. They just keep their promises."

She scrunches her face. "What does that mean? You'll still have those feelings?"

"Stop calling it *feelings*. What did you think would happen, Dr Barry would wave a wand and I wouldn't be a masochist anymore?"

"What will you do?"

"I'll take care of it by myself, like I did before. What did you expect me to do?"

"I hadn't thought that far ahead."

"I'll still be me. I'll be wired the same way."

"Now whenever I go out, I'll think you're hurting yourself."

"Think whatever you want," I say. "I've told you there won't be anyone else. The rest is private, okay?"

"Do you think the sessions are doing us any good?"

I flinch, and hate myself for it.

"I meant with Dr Barry."

"Have I ever missed an appointment?"

"It's not—penance, is it? You really think he can help us?"

"Do *you*?"

The look in her eyes is like wading through a lake, the way the silt gets kicked up. "Ready to turn around?"

We start to walk back. I see our hotel in the distance, its bone-white lamps and purplish interiors exposed. AJ walks slightly ahead of me, holding herself in a bristling, exoskeletal way. I look at her legs, the long blades of her muscles sharpening. I think of the night we met, at this fucking awful party on a roof. She had just come back from Estonia, where she'd been living on a farm.

It was a sort of kibbutz, as far as I could understand, in quite a remote area. There was a bike, and every day she rode into the pine forest. She saw snakes and frogs and rabbits, and creatures she didn't recognize: one that looked like a cowboy hat, and a strange type of deer with stubby legs and big floppy ears. I could see her spacing out as she spoke about it.

At the edge of the forest was a pale green shore, on which cows grazed and drank straight from the sea. She said the Baltic's so dilute the grass grows all the way to its edge. She took off her clothes and swam out. She did this every day. It was autumn. The water was so chilly she could feel her heart beating slower and slower. When it felt like it had almost stopped, she would swim back to the bank and lie on a big flat rock.

One afternoon she was drying on the rock, and she felt a thread of sunlight inside her chest. She had never believed in the existence of a soul except in abstract terms, yet she felt this, and she knew it was her soul. She wasn't planning to do anything with it; she just liked knowing it was there. When she told me this story, I immediately began to picture myself with her, so I never used to like it when she told it to anyone else. Later, I realized no one else understands what the story's about. Everyone seems to think it's about religion, but what it really means is that she knows how to be alone.

When we reach the hotel, she holds the door and gives me a soft look. Her shoulders are gold. We cross the lobby and step into the lift. We turn and face our blurred reflections in the metal doors. I picture myself alone in our flat, eating in front of the TV. The doors open and another couple gets in.

"We're going up," we tell them.

They shrug and smile. They seem Italian. When the lift stops on our floor, we say goodbye to them and walk down the corridor. AJ swipes the key card and we go inside.

The lights come on with a pop. She goes into the bathroom and shuts the door.

I see the bubblebath on the desk, and an image of myself buying it. I look at the mirrored shells of the buildings across the street and listen to the spatter of the shower. The air vent blows on my face, and I start to feel I'm standing by a hotel window in the future, looking back on this night and seeing it compressed into a flash. The water shuts off. I wait for her to come out, her skin steaming.

New Jersey

They're out of breath when they reach Erin's building, but they run up the stairs.

"Ow," Jimmy says, pressing her ribs and laughing. She does track, so this should be nothing, but she smoked two cigarettes at the gig. They get five minutes' grace period before Erin's dad bolts the front door. If they have to ring the bell, Erin's grounded for a fortnight. No negotiating. When they reach the top landing, Erin already has her key out. She turns it in the lock and the door clicks open.

"Phew."

"I know."

They take off their shoes and leave them outside on the rack. The hall light is on and her parents' door is open. Erin goes to talk to them.

Jimmy stops in the bathroom to wash the Sharpie Xs off the backs of her hands. She doesn't have a curfew, but they never stay at hers because she lives up at the far corner of Hoboken and shares a room with little twin sisters who never shut up. Erin lives six blocks from the station and has a queen-size bed. She says Jimmy's lucky, but Jimmy thinks curfews are nice, in a way. It means someone else is the adult.

The ink isn't coming off. Even though Erin didn't get X-ed

tonight, she didn't try to get served; she never risks it unless they're in some nowhere dive. She's honestly the only person Jimmy knows who can pull off a fake ID. At seventeen, Erin looks fourteen, but she always wears a full face of makeup and a push-up bra and dresses neck to toe in black, so the glamour quotient kind of throws it off. Jimmy has never worn a bra of any kind, and she's had her period twice so far. She hopes some of Erin's girlness will rub off on her. She dries her hands and goes to Erin's room.

The walls are covered in Megadeth and Slayer posters, and the floor with tatami matting. They only have it in the bedrooms; the rest of the apartment has the oatmeal-colored carpet with map shapes, like everyone has. Erin's dad teaches Oceanography at Stevens. Their family moved here from Japan when Erin was nine. She and Jimmy were new at school the same year. They were both small for their age and flunking fourth grade, since Erin barely spoke English and Jimmy barely spoke. They used to swap lunches and smile at each other. Though they still trade panda rice balls for PBJ, some things have changed. Jimmy's grown by maybe a foot and a half, Erin aced the mock SATs, and they're metalheads now.

Tonight they saw Maiden play the Ritz, though they told Erin's parents it was Pearl Jam. Occasionally Erin's dad, who goes to Trinity Lutheran, flips out and rips up Erin's band posters, and Erin gets really mad and depressed. Then her mom, who's a Buddhist, buys her all new ones and she's allowed to keep them for a while.

Erin comes in and turns on the paper lamp by her bed and moves it down next to Jimmy. She clicks off the overhead light and kisses Bruce Dickinson on one of the band posters.

"I want to have your babies," she tells him. She locks the door and slides under her bed like a car mechanic. "Can you believe they played *four* encores?"

"Yah, epic," Jimmy says.

Erin emerges with the small flat bottle of vodka and two shot glasses she keeps taped to the underside of the bedsprings. She pulls off all the tape and pours them each a shot. Normally she carries a hipflask and when they come back from the city, they go to the park on the pier to drink and look across the water at where they've been, but she knew they'd get frisked at the concert.

They clink glasses and Jimmy takes a sip. Erin knocks the whole thing back and doesn't even pull a face. She really likes to drink, and she taught Jimmy how. *Once you realize it isn't meant to taste good, it starts to taste good.* She tops off Jimmy's glass, pours herself another and tosses it back. She takes off her jacket and stretches out on the floor. She has a perfect peanut body, small and tanned and curvy.

Whenever Jimmy says she's bored, Erin says, *Wanna make out?* and Jimmy says, *Sure.* They laugh but sometimes Jimmy imagines how it would be. She's not a dyke, right—she tested it. There's a magazine in the staff bathroom at work, and the pictures make her wet, but if she checks out real girls in the locker room, she doesn't feel a thing. And it's not like she loves Erin or wants to date her. It's more because she's almost seventeen and has never done anything and girls just seem so much cleaner. When Jimmy needs to make herself come, she can never imagine it with a guy. She has to pretend another girl's body is in front of her body and she's kissing her neck and feeling her tits and rubbing her, instead of herself. It's not Erin, but it could be Erin. Plus Erin has a sort-of boyfriend, which makes it definitely not gay.

Jimmy closes her eyes and tips her drink down her throat, feeling her stomach close like a fist. She tucks her knees to her chest and hugs them.

"So if I had your eyes and height, but my body and mouth," Erin is saying, "and I grew my hair down to there, and had bangs, but not stupid ones, then guys would have to look at me."

"They look at you now," Jimmy says.

"And I want a real ass. I have a flat ass." Erin rolls onto her stomach and pours herself another shot. She downs it, arching her back, and wipes her mouth with her knuckles. "Well, okay, it's not so much flat as low. I think it dropped when I had mono. All I did was lay in bed for like a year. I lost hella muscle tone."

"It looks good that way. Like an upside-down heart."

"Hmm," Erin says. She sits up and fills their glasses. "I can't believe they didn't play 'Killers'."

"Or 'Seventh Son of a Seventh Son'."

Erin sings the guitar riff. There's a tap on the door. Jimmy's nearer the bed, so she shoves her shot glass and the bottle underneath it. Erin downs hers, drops the glass down her top, and reaches up to turn the doorknob so the button pops out. "It's open," she calls, winking at Jimmy.

"Go to sleep," her mom says through the door.

"Okay." Erin reaches over and turns off the lamp.

"Good night, Jimmy," Erin's mom says.

"Oh, night Mrs Ando."

They crawl into bed and stifle their giggles until they hear the door close at the end of the hall.

"Tonight was the best," Erin whispers, sitting up and pulling her shirt up over her head.

Staying under the blanket, Jimmy takes off her jeans and

drops them on the floor. She isn't wearing anything under her tank top so she leaves it on.

Erin lays back down. "Don't you hate how just when our lives are getting good, we're going to be split up?"

"We have a whole year," Jimmy says, "and we'll always be friends."

"It'll be different after high school. We'll have totally different lives."

"Our lives are different now, and we're still best friends."

"You know what I mean. I'll be at college, and you'll be in the army."

"But then we'll both have jobs and we'll be the same again," Jimmy says. In the darkness she can see the white of Erin's bra. "You know I still have my shot under the bed."

"Wanna split it?"

"You have it." Jimmy folds her arms behind her head. "I have work tomorrow. I'm worried I'll smell."

"Vodka doesn't have a smell."

"It does. It's sweet."

Erin crawls to the bottom of the bed, does the shot, and crawls back up. She lays right against Jimmy's side.

"We'll make it the best year," Jimmy tells her. "We'll go to all the gigs."

"Yah. White Zombie's playing the Plaza New Year's Eve. And Pantera's touring, but I don't know if they have New York dates."

"It doesn't matter," Jimmy says, "we can go out of state. One of the waitresses just had a baby, and me and this other girl are splitting her shifts until she comes back. I'll be able to buy my car by the end of summer." She can smell Erin's conditioner.

"Cool," Erin says, wriggling away and turning to face her.

"But aww, that means we won't get to hang out. I wish you worked around here, so I could come see you."

"It's Jersey City, not the moon. But if you come, bring a book or something. I won't have time to entertain you."

"Fine." Erin sounds miffed.

Jimmy hadn't meant to be so peevish, but Erin just doesn't get it. Work isn't like school, where nothing is real and nothing you do has any effect on the world. People yell at Jimmy when she messes up. The chef threw a spatula at her head. Besides, she prefers working in the Heights where hardly anyone from school ever comes in, and if they do they're shopping with their mother or something, so it's more humiliating for them.

"Come for dinner sometime," Jimmy says to make up. "It's fancy. We have candles and stuff. Bring what's-his-face." Erin's boyfriend is called Hayden Pipes. He goes to The Hudson School with all the other preppy dicks. Erin met him at church.

"Oh!" Erin says. "I can't believe I haven't told you."

"What?"

"We did it."

"What? When?"

"Thursday."

"God," Jimmy says. Of all the people in the world Erin could have given it up to, Hayden Pipes is the least deserving. Jimmy's almost certain he plucks his eyebrows. "How am I supposed to cover for you if you don't tell me when you're seeing him?"

"No, Thursday day," Erin says, "I didn't have to say where I was."

"In the daytime?"

"Yeah, so?"

"Gross."

"Why is it gross?"

"I can't believe you didn't tell me."

"I'm telling you now."

"We've been hanging out all night."

"Only at the best gig in the world," Erin says. "It's not that big a deal. You'll see. The earlier stuff changes you more. This is just one step further."

It's annoying when Erin pretends to be all wise and womanly, but Jimmy wants information more than she wants to fight. "Did it hurt?"

"Mm-hm."

"A lot or just a little?"

"A lot, kinda. I don't know." Erin was much more excited when she told Jimmy about sixty-nine.

"Was there blood?"

"Some."

"But did it feel good though?"

"It was better when he ate me out."

"Will you do it again?"

"Maybe not, if it was up to me. But it seems like once we've done it, then that's what we're doing, you know?"

"Are you sure you didn't get pregnant?"

"Oh no," Erin says, "he didn't come inside me."

Jimmy's face feels hot. "Outside? Everywhere, like in magazines? On your tits?"

"Yeah."

"You liked that?"

"Um, yeah. It's kind of neat."

Jimmy doesn't get it. He's not even Erin's type. He doesn't have long hair or play the guitar. She realizes Erin is waiting for her to say something. "Okay. I mean, it sounds great. Really."

"You sound mad."

Jimmy hadn't thought she was mad, but as soon as Erin says that, she starts to feel furious. "Why would I be mad?"

"I don't know. Why are you?"

"I'm not."

"You are, you're totally losing your shit," Erin says. It sounds like she's smiling. "You're jealous because I'm an adult, and you're just—you're *scared*."

"Give me a break," Jimmy says. "You're an adult? Because you fucked some idiotic guy?"

"Hey," Erin says. "Stop."

"I pay taxes. I'm buying a car. No one's helping me. Your parents still give you pocket money."

"Why are we fighting about this?" Erin says.

"We're not."

"Oh, okay. We're not."

The pitch of their voices hangs in the air, getting louder and louder in Jimmy's head. She and Erin don't argue very often, but when they do, it's always on the phone or in the dark. It's as if they can only hurt each other when they can't see the other person's face. In their friendship, Erin's the leader. She's the winner as well as the loser: she always has the last word in a fight, but she's also the one who apologizes first, no matter who's to blame. It feels like this time might be different.

It seems very quiet. Jimmy turns over and sniffs Erin's hair. Erin never snores and her breathing doesn't change when she's asleep, but you can always tell when she's crashed by her scent, of baking bread. Jimmy rolls onto her back and pulls the covers up to her chin. She closes her eyes and pictures the hot magic of the candy-lit rock club, as cloudy as heaven.

She dreams of a house in the desert. The scorched yellow grass pokes through her socks as she walks across the back yard, carrying a trash bag and rubbing it to get the layers to come apart. Shiny objects are scattered around the yard. She finds a pair of welding goggles and a set of pliers. A Bowie knife. It's like a video game, she doesn't have to pick them up, has only to walk nearby to absorb them. The items follow her, hovering at the border of her vision. At the edge of the yard is a big tree stump with a dead, wet squirrel lying on it, and a bucket of water with bits of fur floating on top.

She puts on the goggles and tightens the strap. She flips the squirrel onto its stomach and makes an incision in its back. Hooking her index fingers into the slit, she yanks them apart so the skin tears all the way around. It's in two pieces, like a shirt and pants. Her hands are slippery.

With the pliers, she snaps the ankle and wrist bones and twists off the boy parts. She cuts around the wrists and neck and slips off the top half of the skin like a pullover with the head and the hands still attached. She swirls the knife in the bucket before sawing off the feet and the tail. When she tries to take off the pants, there are stringy bits at the bottom that she has to sever.

She arranges the skinless body on the tree stump and wipes her goggles with her sleeve. Presses the tip of the knife against the pelvis and slides it up across the abdomen. At the bottom of the ribcage, she works the blade in deeper and slices to the throat. She opens the ribcage with her thumbs and gently scoops out the guts, careful not to squash the gall bladder. If it bursts, it will ruin the meat. Cutting out the heart and lungs before she pulls out the windpipe, she breaks the pelvis with the pliers, poking out the last of the innards and a few black pellets with her pinky.

Her socks are bloody. She peels them off and drops them in the trash bag. She uncoils the garden hose and opens the faucet. It must be near noon; the house casts no shadow. She washes her hands and face and rinses the body. She can't remember what time he said he wanted to eat. She shuts off the water and goes up the porch steps.

His truck isn't here. She opens the screen door and walks into the house. On TV is an advertisement for candy. A girl is eating it and laughing. Jimmy stares at the headless red body on the cutting board, trying to work out what day of the week it is. She chops off the arms and the legs and saws the torso in half. She arranges the pieces in a Pyrex dish and rifles through the drawers, looking for cellophane wrap. She still has to clean up all that stuff in the yard. He hates to see a mess. She mixes salt and tap water in a glass and pours it over the meat. Do they have any buttermilk? When she opens the fridge, it's crammed with Barbie dolls. Their hair is long and cold and shiny.

She swallows, tasting seawater. The hot blue light of the clock punctures the darkness. She's balled on her side with tears in her mouth, a scared, sick feeling twisting in her veins. Something about Erin's radiating cottony warmth makes it worse. Jimmy gets up and tugs on her jeans, buttoning them as she slips out of the room. She pads through the dark, silent apartment and lets herself out. The lights on the landing flicker as she puts on her shoes. She hurries down the stairs and pushes open the heavy glass door, drops of water strung like necklaces on the pane.

The streets are black mirrors reflecting the burning shells of the sodium lamps, the buildings dark-eyed in the soft blond light. The night air touches her face as she turns the corner and walks toward the pier, and she tastes the smell of tin cans that comes, always, after rain.

Transformer

You're new. You sit next to me in Maths. Mr Chapman asks you why your homework's so messy, why all the numbers are falling out of the squares. You say you live on a houseboat and the sea is choppy at night. You have thick, dark hair, and big hands. I picture you asleep, your bed rocking.

People say the first one is the one you'll love forever, so I pop my cherry with a Coke bottle before inviting myself over. I duck into your swaying cabin, its low ceiling lined with movie posters. We take gold sips from a silver flask and you bite your mouth and look at me. We dry hump to a documentary about Stonehenge.

At the movies you slip me an E, and the taxi takes off like a plane. We drink the harbor lights and eat the salty air. The moon is a prince and our thoughts are sunbursts. As we glide through the streets, the city twists her body around us. She has peeling billboard skin and bamboo bones. Her eyes are scraped skies reflected in glass, her hair waving tendrils of factory smoke. The club is her neon-lit heart, throbbing music and color. Flames melt the ends of our straws and the bass makes our teeth crumble.

In the multi-storey car park you spread your jacket beside a silver Jaguar. I lie down and pull my necklace to the side. You keep staring into my eyes, so I turn my head and look at a disc of oil pinned beneath a tire. With each passing car, an arm of light reaches under the chassis to clock me in the eyes, and bands of color scroll across the oil. There's a metal rod attached to your spine I can feel through your skin.

Summer comes, and with it long afternoons on warm white sheets, memorizing your mouth. You touch my nipples as day squeezes through the blinds. I suck until your eyes change color. On the way to the beach your hair gets blonder. It feels waxy against my lips. We read to one another from a creased paperback, the pages thick and damp, our bodies sugared with sand. I wrap my legs around you in the water and when you get close, you pull out.

On the red-eye, you smile and your teeth are smaller. You still smell like sunshiny hair. In the seat pockets in front of us are two versions of the same book. You don't know that, since the alphabets are different. I decide not to tell you. You look at my mouth as you take off your tie and unfasten a button. Your thumbs are double-jointed and your nails mooned and shiny. When the lights go down, I touch your knee. You roll up your sleeves and lift the armrest, fitting your fingers inside me. The in-flight movie flickers in your eyes.

You kneel on the quad. Your hair is longer and floppier. You tuck it behind your ears, opening your sketchbook to an eye that takes up the whole page. The lashes are lines from songs, written in cursive. I ask you for a tattoo. Your pen tickles my arm. I jog down the trail by flashlight. You're waiting by the river, your cheeks creased from sleep. The ground is cold and lunar so we do it on all fours. You kiss my neck the whole time. Your mouth blazes like a sun.

On the first night of Christmas vacation, I wake up in your sister's room. I can smell something burning. I go to the kitchen. You're back from basic training and you're buttering toast. I picture you doing push-ups in mud, a boot on your shoulder. Your head's shaved and it feels like emery paper. We get up from the floor, brushing off crumbs.

We robodose at Disneyland, and you sit with your sister on the Peter Pan ride. Flying over the tiny lights of London, I see a miniature version of myself standing on a rooftop. We spend the whole afternoon on the Small World ride, singing at the top of our voices and thinking we're actually in all of the places. You show me that the clouds look different in every country. The mysteries of the cosmos unfold in the Electric Light Parade.

I tiptoe down the hall. You take off your T-shirt and toss it over the lamp. You unbutton your jeans and throw me on the bed, going fast and deep. My eyes blink. You've gotten thicker. You drag me to the edge, where you hold my thighs and fuck me standing. I like the way your buckle hits my butt. When the weather warms, we start meeting by the river again. You have a new thing, cupping my ass in your hands and lifting me up to your mouth. We get stoned in a practice room and play the piano. The heat makes us slow. We lie on our backs, the boat tipping side to side, books splayed around us like spent lovers.

At night, we climb the fence. Lost in the dark, we snap photos of the tombstones to illuminate them. The statues of angels and crosses glimmer in the flash. We've used up the film by the time we find the grave of the rock singer. We get on our knees and I pray my life won't be ordinary, while you pray that yours will. You run your tongue down my stomach and I tug your hair that's grown back thick and wiry. Sunlight slopes through the low windows of your cabin onto the dented sheets.

The pictures come back beautiful. We go to the punk bar to score pills from the bouncer. We dance beneath a railway arch, alone with the universe in a smoke-marbled shaft of lilac light, our hearts flatlining with the breakdown, the drums re-patterning our DNA. You skin up on the bed. We swap clothes and draw each other, passing the joint. Your shirt's warm and sweaty and your stubble scrapes my lips. You have my dress on with the zip open at the back. I push it up your thighs. I take you out of my knickers and swallow you whole. You want me on top, touching my tits. You're a talker.

I put a spliff in your mouth and light it. In the flare, your hair appears sun-kissed, your eyes more dilute. You slip your hand in my back pocket as we dance to the band. You give me a blowback. You pick the cinders off your tongue and tie my wrists to the bed frame. You live near the airport. I hear the scream of jet engines as you fuck me from behind. Your mouth and breasts brush my back and your bone is plastic. We draw each other in the bath. You have a black eye that requires a lot of shading.

Your studio's across the field and down the street from mine. It used to be swimming baths, and the twinkling, hazy light bouncing off the tile makes it feel as if it's still submerged. You paint from Polaroids, and when we kiss, you smell of turps. For Valentine's we do trips with pink hearts. You've had your nipple pierced and the barbell clicks against my teeth. No matter how I try, I can't make you come. I'm holding your hair so you can do a line, but you're crying too hard.

You stand by the bar, talking to me while I clean the coffee machine. It takes me a while to recognize you without the lectern. Your wife is tiny perfection and doesn't move her hips when you fuck her next to me, but works her jaw, as if coaching a fussy eater. It's her beauty versus my youth. We cancel each other out great.

You've shaved your head again, and started playing the bass with an armful of tattoos. You're enraged in a sexy sort of way, and you always want to do it doggy-style. It only bothers me because you have a dog. You want me to give up meat and milk. You take the rubber off without telling me. You tell me I'm too manufactured, whatever that means.

You score pills in the back room and we leave the drinks thing early. You take me to a building you used to work in, and we ride a glass rocket to the roof. I look up into the night sky and see a huge Peter Pan galleon floating by. You drop the needle onto the record, and the bedroom starts spinning. We stretch out on the carpet and turn to each other, halo-eyed. When you touch me, your face is a perfect mash of sadness and bliss. I feel an unfamiliar ache.

We move into a flat overlooking a prison that's concreted over, with pieces of glass jutting out. We drink Ricard on the balcony, in the sun. I press last number redial, and speak to quite a young-sounding prostitute who says she knows how to choke people. When I look out of the window, I think of a giant sleeping reptile with glittering scales. The pills are laced with acid that doesn't hit until I'm coming down, watching your face as you fuck me. With every stroke, you turn into a different animal. Every animal you become is an animal you already are.

The needle's bouncing. I like its thumping heart, but you get up to change the record. You say you're a different person. I think you're the same.

Would Like to Meet

t was eight-thirty and I was trying to close the shop, but people kept tapping on the windows and begging me to unlock the door. They pulled faces and mimed praying hands. I let them in, wondering what they could possibly need so much. It's a gift shop; nothing there is life or death. They selected wine glasses, bricks of granular soap, and those snap-crotched leotards that babies wear.

I scratched off the price stickers, stuck them to my arm and wrapped the items. My fingertips were sweaty and the tissue paper stained them hot pink. The sticky tape split as I pulled it off the roll, and I'd needed to pee since the first flotilla of 9-to-5ers had stepped off the train. I crammed everything into crunchy, twine-handled paper bags and rang the prices off my arm, running payments on the card machine and feigning total interest in the pattern of the floor tile while people keyed their pins.

A businessman approached the till with a pair of earrings and a card with "SORRY" stamped across the front. I thought the quotes made it seem sarcastic, but retail's all about keeping your mouth shut, like at Valentine's, when it's better not to mention that hearts signify vaginas. People lingered by the jewelry cabinets, hugging their purchases and stroking their lips. I swept the floor, trying to push them out with the power of thought. Someone drifted into the toiletries section to finger the bath bombs. People twirled the greeting card racks.

They kept coming. A woman clawed the glass like a hungry zombie. When I let her in, she phoned someone and started making her way around the shop, describing every item in slightly disparaging terms. When the other person didn't approve of any of the suggestions, she started getting ratty. I hole-punched a sheaf of invoices and started filing them. The phone conversation ended in a row, and the woman stormed out. She left the door wide open and as I went to close it, another woman came running into the shop. She made a dash for the photo frames. I locked the door and did more paperwork. The metal claws of the files snapped shut. I opened the post.

When she'd made up her mind, she made me tear up the stock room to find one with the cellophane still on the box, and then she had me take it off, because she wanted a picture placed inside before I wrapped it. Times like this, I missed waitressing. People would notice if I spat on their gifts. She handed me a photograph of her and a man with a beard that went all the way up to his eyes on the Champs-Élysées. They looked disproportionately thrilled about being next to one another in France. The photo was twice the size of the frame.

"You can cut him out," she said, rubbing his face with her finger. "This is for someone else."

I found the scissors and trimmed it down to size. The frame came with a slick, filmy insert of a male model with feathered hair and a bow-tie mouth, and his sweater sleeves pushed up. I replaced it with hers. Putting the Styrofoam corners back on, I repackaged the frame and wrapped it and rang up the sale. As the customer typed her pin number, I looked at the fake boyfriend picture. That man was probably someone's boyfriend in real life. His girlfriend could buy this frame and use it straight out of the box.

The customer left. I yanked the shutter halfway down, locked the glass door and ran to the bathroom, but by then I'd been holding it so long that I didn't need to go anymore. I squizzled floor cleaner into the bucket, put it in the sink, and opened the hot water tap. I went out front and dimmed the lights and stuck a tape in the deck. I X-ed the till, glancing at the CCTV screen as I stapled together the petty cash slips. There was still a customer in the back. I sighed and went through.

"Hi, sorry, we're closed."

Army backpack, dirty jeans. I knew another ex-art student when I saw one. He was tall and pudgy and fair, with invisible eyebrows and flushed skin. He held up a music box. "How much?"

"Thirty-four ninety-nine."

"It's my girlfriend's birthday," he said.

I didn't think so. Blackheads coated his nose. They were long and pointed, like hair. Any female presence in his life would have yanked those babies out with a Bioré strip by now. I didn't understand the purpose of the lie, but I was too tired to care.

"Okay," I said. I hoped he would have found something by the time I finished mopping the floor. I went to get the bucket, and as I closed the tap, I felt him come up behind me. He wrapped his arm around my neck, pushing something against my bra clasp. When he repositioned it higher, I felt a hard point poking through the back of my shirt. He was shaking, and he smelled bad. I wished I'd gone to the bathroom before.

"Do exactly as I say."

I noticed his precise diction and well-spoken accent. I wondered what had gone wrong in his life. As he pushed me to the front of the shop, I looked through the window at the minicab office across the road. The owner always leans against the doorway, chewing a toothpick and watching me in a skeezy way. Where the hell was he now? When we reached the till, I glanced at the X-read. Everyone pays by card, so there was only eighty in cash, plus the float. I hit NO SALE. When the drawer leapt out, I blocked his view with my body, pawing the money into the backpack and throwing in the credit card slips, discarded change bags, and counterfeit detector pen to make it seem fuller. I tightened the drawstring before passing it back over my shoulder.

"On the floor," he said. "Count to a hundred."

I got down on the tile and clasped my hands over my head. I waited for him to leave. He stood there for a while, and then he sat on top of me. It seemed improvised, as if he'd been planning to leave and something had changed his mind. He was squashing my lungs and I couldn't breathe properly. I heard a clicking sound I recognized right away as the sound of a box-cutter blade adjusting. The point dug into the soft place behind my ear.

"Are you going to hurt me?" I said. My voice had come out in a whisper, and I wasn't sure if he'd heard. Maybe he didn't know. The tip of the blade punctured my skin.

When he shifted his weight, I tensed my body, visualizing how to push him off, twist round, and make a grab for the box-cutter, but he planted a knee in the middle of my back and wrapped my hair around his fist. He made a small incision at the base of my neck, near the hairline. It burned instead of hurt. He held still, and I thought he was looking at it.

He seemed to get lighter, and a strange idea flitted across my mind. I thought it was the weight of his soul leaving his body, and that he wasn't all there anymore. I got really scared then. I didn't think he wanted to kill me, but to destroy me in some other way.

I knew what was required, an ultimate act of salesmanship, but I couldn't think of a single good thing I'd done or might do. I have friends, none of them close, and no immediate family. I lost my parents in a car accident when I was seven, and my grandmother raised me. She died when I was eighteen. I decided to invent a fiancé and a baby, but when I opened my mouth, a different story came out.

"I'm a failure. I've never done anything worthwhile or interesting. I'm necessary to no one. Please don't make it worse." I changed my breathing and tried to cry.

I felt my hair unwinding from around his hand. He got up. The change in the backpack jangled and his soles squeaked against the tile. I heard him unlock the door and bang his head against the lip of the shutter on his way out. I stood up and looked at the empty drawer for a while before I closed it. I touched the cut as I waited for the Z-read to print off. I looked at my hand. I wanted a fish finger sandwich with ketchup. I didn't want to have to talk to anyone. I checked the printout and went across the road to the cashpoint. I withdrew a hundred and ninety pounds from my savings account, and replaced the float and the takings. I threw out the mop water and set the alarm. It beeped as I pulled the shutter down and slid in the locks.

I walked around the corner and up the street to my house, thinking about what I'd said to the robber. This was the second thing that had happened to me that day. After lunch, a woman had come in with a small girl in a sailor dress. She was the kind of child who's more interested in how the shop works than in any of the merchandise. She stood by the counter, watching me wrap items for a customer who was still browsing. The kids who come in think of it as a toyshop, even though we sell lots of other things, and I thought she probably envied me the way I used to envy the ice-cream man. I didn't care that she was only a kid. I liked feeling good about my job, for a change.

"So," she said, brushing her hair out of her eyes, "is this your life job? I mean, is this what you're going to do for the rest of your life?"

"I hope not," I said, and tried to laugh it off.

I cast around for her mother to come and shut her down, but she was engrossed in the linen handkerchiefs embroidered by Bulgarian widows. The girl eyed me.

"Um, I have a degree," I said. "I went to art school."

"Then why aren't you an artist?"

"I wanted to be a real artist, but something happened. My confidence failed. These days, I'm more of an illustrator. But you have to put yourself out there, and I'm not very good at that."

She gave me a cool stare.

"I illustrated a pub menu. I've sold a few drawings on Etsy."

She tipped her head to the side. "That sounds quite good."

"Listen," I said, "I'll give you ten pounds every time you come in here and question me about my life."

She twisted her mouth. "Are you married? Have you got a boyfriend?"

"Perfect. Exactly like that."

She opened her hand and placed it on the counter.

"Starting from next time. Today's the audition."

She seemed crestfallen, so I gave her a faulty faux-Japanese doll from behind the till. All the girls her age are crazy about them. My flatmate Sachiko told me Japanese people have these dolls in their houses if they've lost a baby, and someone must have copied them without knowing what they meant. I liked the original idea. I thought there could be different dolls standing in for the different things that have been lost.

It was Friday night. Everyone was out. I went to the bathroom and put a few plasters on my neck. I thought if my life was a movie, this was when I'd decide to be artificially inseminated, open a cake-making business, or cycle across South America. I put a bun in the toaster oven and slid the fish fingers under the grill. I couldn't think of a single thing I wanted to do apart from quitting the shop.

That would just mean having to look for something else. I've already worked at the video shop, the normal pub, the racist pub, and the Italian restaurant opposite the Cypriot car wash. Since I don't know how to cut hair or fry chicken, there's nothing else for me around here, and I shouldn't have to commute for the kind of money I make.

I could probably get a better job, in an office or something, if I took out a few of my piercings and covered my chest piece. I never needed any of this before, because I used to be the real thing, an artist. It felt like I was carrying a kind of light inside me all the time. My first year of art school, the light went out. Almost overnight, I became deeply ordinary. It was a kind of paralysis. I didn't even have the momentum to drop out, so I concealed the absence of an artist with the image of one. This is all I have left of that part of me.

The sesame seeds were singed. I built the sandwich, squirted a fjord of ketchup onto the plate and took it into the living room. There was a new *Time Out*, and I flicked through it as I ate. My favorite part is the personals, especially the stories of missed connections, and I like the alternative lifestyles section because of the direct way people describe themselves and what they want.

PROFESSIONAL COUPLE caught my eye because it struck me as funny, as if being together was their job. I read on: 30S, INTO CAMPING, HIKING. I wondered if this was some new-fangled party-and-play slang. I tried to guess what the terms could mean. Hiking sounded like it might be sexy. SEEKING CONSCIOUS, N/S FEMALE FOR SOMETHING REAL. LONDON.

I cleaned the tub and ran a bath. I sat in the water, crying about my day. I brushed my teeth and tried to watch a movie on my laptop. I had to rewind the opening scene a few times, because my mind kept drifting. Something real. It totally threw me. Either they were saying it wasn't all about sex, or it was and it would be mind-blowing. I decided the good thing about finding out you had nothing and wanted nothing, was that you had nothing to lose. I went out to the living room. My housemates were back from the pub. They asked me about my day. Fine, I said, and took the magazine to my room. I sat on my bed and read the ad again before dialing the number. I typed in the code.

"Hi." It was a woman's voice. "Er—maybe you could tell us a bit about yourself. Okay. Thanks. We're Jack and Amber."

I opted to listen to the greeting again. Her voice was warm and hard, like her name. The tone beeped. I still didn't know what they wanted, so I wasn't sure how to pitch it.

"Hello? I'm Vivien Chiang. I don't smoke. I'm conscious if you meant it in the biological sense. I've never done anything like this before, but I had a terrible day at work. I guess you didn't need to know that, but anyway. The wording of your advert intrigued me. I'm open for something new."

I left my number and ended the call. I went back to watching the movie. I knew I'd sounded crazy, but if I entered a re-recording spiral, it could get expensive. A little while later, my phone played the girls' chorus from "Walk on the Wild Side". I paused the film and found my phone on the bed.

HI VIVIEN. DINNER SATURDAY? AMBER

DEFINITELY, I texted back.

WHERE DO U LIVE

SE LONDON. U?

I waited.

WEST. WE KNOW A PLACE NEAR U

OK GREAT

CAN PICK U UP AT YRS

I texted the address and said I'd be ready at eight.

On Saturday after work, I ran back to the house and took a shower. I always come back covered in glitter, even if I'm sure I haven't touched any. I didn't think anyone was home, but when I passed Sachiko's room, I saw her lying on her bed, reading a book. I adjusted my towel before going in.

"Heya," she said, extending a packet of gummy bears.

"I need help."

"Sure," she said. "Anything."

"I have a date in fifteen minutes, and I have nothing to wear. Just anything is fine."

She got up and opened her wardrobe. She pulled out a bunch of dresses by their hangers and draped them over my arms.

"Thanks. I don't know, can I take you out for a beer in the week?"

"I'd like that," she said. "Have fun."

I went to my room and piled them on the bed. I took off the towel and sprayed perfume on my wrists and the backs of my knees. It was five to eight. There wasn't time to try everything on, so I held each dress against my body in front of the mirror. They were simple designs in lush, evocative shades, and felt dreamlike against my skin. I put on a midnight blue dress and black high-heeled shoes. The chorus of girls announced a text.

WE'RE HERE

I shrugged on my bomber jacket, breathing its good, animal smell, zipped my keys, phone and debit card into the pocket, and clopped out of the house. There was a black car parked on the corner, and as I tottered towards it, I could see them. They were better looking and younger than I'd expected, perhaps five or six years older than me. I climbed into the back and scooted to the middle. They both poked their heads around their seats at the same time.

Amber had a mournful, sensuous face with pretty, purplish crescents under her eyes, and dark hair laced into a side plait. She looked at me through her eyelashes like a Modigliani. Jack was an Egon Schiele, with classical features edged by a deranged sort of beauty. His light brown hair had a golden cast. We shook hands. Amber's grip was firmer than Jack's.

"There's this cute brasserie in Crystal Palace with Frenchy sort of food," she said. "Does that sound fine?"

"Sure. Great."

When Jack started the car, Amber turned to face the front. "I have to look at the road," she said. Her hand touched the dash. She had long fingers, pink polish that was almost white, a silver wedding band.

"What do you do, Vivien?" Jack said, tipping his head back as he looked at me in the rearview mirror. He had small, deep-set, gray eyes and starry eyelashes.

"I work in a shop, but I trained as an illustrator."

"Interesting," Amber said. "You know, Jack designs fonts."

"Really?" I poked my head between the seats. "How about you, Amber?"

"I'm a curator at the V&A."

"That's my favorite museum," I said.

"I'm glad."

I could smell Jack's aftershave. I leaned back and looked out the window.

We parked on the corner and walked up the street. The restaurant was all black wood and bright brass. A girl took our coats and the maître d' scanned his roster. Amber had a tight little body wrapped in black jeans and a deconstructed Doors tee. I thought we had both dressed the way the other person normally did. The maître d' led us to a small, glass-encased room near the back of the restaurant. It looked like somewhere you'd plan a war. The whole idea was to have the ambience without the noise, but it had the opposite effect. The glass didn't reach the ceiling, so the noise drifted in anyway, and the darkened restaurant turned the glass into a mirror. Amber sat opposite me and Jack sat next to her. We smiled and picked up our menus.

"Cute dress," Amber said.

"It isn't mine."

"You should steal it."

I peered at them over the top of my menu and pictured us having a three-way. I'd never been with anyone older than me. That there were two of them made me feel safe. When the waiter appeared I wasn't ready, but they were, so I ordered the same thing as Amber. He took our menus and left.

"Have you always lived in London?" I asked Amber.

"I grew up in Colchester," she said. "I came here to study. Jack's from London."

"Sort of," Jack said. "I was born in Golders Green, but I spent most of my childhood overseas. My parents were diplomats. They're retired and divorced now."

"Mine never married," Amber said. "They're teachers."

"And you?" Jack said.

"East London, until I was seven. When my parents died, I went to live with my grandmother in Brixton."

"Oh no," Amber said.

"It's not as bad as it sounds."

The drinks arrived. As Jack took the straws out of his drink, I noticed his beautiful spatula fingers and square nails.

"How did the two of you meet?" I asked.

"It was the weirdest thing," Amber said. "We sat next to each other on a flight into Heathrow. We didn't swap numbers or anything. Three days later, I bumped into him on the street."

"Sounds like it was meant to be. How long have you been married?"

"I can never remember," Amber said, turning to Jack.

"Nine years," he said. "We don't have kids."

I told them the story of how I'd hired a kid as my life coach. They both laughed at my little jokes, and it felt good. It turned out we'd all been to art school, so we talked about that for a while. We discussed the Turner nominees, the films of Matthew Barney, and a Rebecca Horn exhibition we'd all seen. I decided I was more physically drawn to Jack and more psychologically attracted to Amber. She had a sexier manner, and I thought her reasons for wanting to do this were probably more complex than his.

When the food arrived, they each put half of their food on the other person's plate. People only do that if they're madly in love. It means they want to experience all the same things, no matter how insignificant. I didn't understand what they thought they needed me for. We talked about books and movies, and books that had been turned into movies. Jack expressed his views in a dominant manner, while Amber was subtly persuasive. Whenever I spoke, they both listened in a serious, attentive way that made me think they were after more than a casual hook-up. By now, I was very curious about what they wanted, but I never address a delicate matter directly. That's the Chinese part of me.

Over coffee, I asked whether they'd had a lot of responses to the advert.

"Quite a few," Amber said, stirring sugar into her latte, "but everyone except for you seemed to think this was exclusively about sex."

"I wasn't sure," I said. "To be honest, I was interested either way."

Amber smiled, and Jack peered into his espresso.

I sipped my coffee.

"So this is mostly about you and Jack," Amber said.

"I understand," I said.

I didn't understand. If she wasn't part of the mix, why had she involved herself at all? The thought crossed my mind that perhaps Jack was chronically unfaithful, and this was Amber's way of exercising control, but I didn't sense that dynamic between them.

"Do you think you'd like to see each other again?" She said it like a mother arranging a play date.

Jack flashed his teeth at me.

"Uh, sure," I said.

"How about you?" she asked him.

"Yes," he said, looking me in the eye.

"Oh, thanks," I said, embarrassed that I was embarrassed. I looked at Amber.

"Great," she said. "You two go out a couple of times, see how it goes. If you hit it off, then I'll start seeing you, too."

I didn't understand why she was leaving the choice up to him, when she would be dating me, too.

She leaned across the table. "So we'd have our own thing," she said. "I don't know if you were expecting this to be all three of us together, but that's not what we're looking for."

I blushed. "I don't know what I was expecting."

She was right. I found the idea of dating them separately a little bit creepy. I could see the fun of a three-way, but conducting parallel affairs seemed obviously to be a twisted game between the two of them. Perhaps they wanted to exchange stories, or never to speak of it, just to know it was something they shared. Whatever it was, it seemed willfully perverse and destructive. I didn't want to be their fetish object, or connective tissue. This crazy thing that happened to them once.

"I should explain," Amber said to Jack. I could feel his mood change as he nodded and turned away.

"We've never even thought about doing anything like this before," she said.

"Okay."

"I have bone cancer."

"My God," I said. I touched my napkin. "I'm so sorry." I looked at Jack.

"I had it when I was a child," Amber said, "and again as a teenager. I don't want to bog you down with the details, but it doesn't look like they can turn things around this time."

"I'm sorry," I said again.

She shook her head and smiled. "I've beaten it twice. That's a lot of bonus time."

Jack fake-coughed.

"I don't get how it connects," I said.

"I need to know he'll find someone else," Amber said, "and I want to meet her."

They looked at each other. There was so much going on in their faces that I had to look away. I understood. They were trying to pull the future into the present, to make a place for Amber in it. I thought it was a beautiful idea. I've always admired people who try to make a good thing last forever. But when I thought about what they were asking of me, it seemed like a big responsibility. We'd only just met. It was too much.

We settled the bill and left the restaurant. A private blanket of sadness wrapped around them on the way to the car. Amber drove. No one spoke. When we stopped in front of the house, she leaned between the seats and kissed me on the cheek. We thanked each other, said we'd be in touch. Jack didn't turn around.

The next day was Sunday. The shop was quiet. I couldn't stop thinking about them. I knew this was my chance to have something written in stone. Everyone who has to love me is gone, and here was someone who would never be able to leave me. Here were two, willing to bend time and space, and the rules, for each other. I thought I could do a lot worse. As I cashed up and mopped the floor, I began to picture museum afternoons and picnics in the park. I pulled down the shutter, slid in the locks, and walked up the road to the house. It was still light.

I went inside and started filling the bath. The magazine was on top of the cistern. I locked the door and read the advert again. I got naked and was just about to step into the bath when I heard singing coming from the floor. I found my phone in my jeans.

It was Amber. "Can you talk?"

"Sure." I was cold and I wanted to get in the water.

"We had a lovely time with you the other night. We both really like you. If it was going to be anyone, it would be you."

"Oh," I said, guarding my expression even though she couldn't see it.

"It's Jack, he's never been fully on board. He was trying to do it for me, but going out the other night made it too real."

"Okay." I wondered if I just hadn't been a good fit.

"He prefers to let things take their natural course. I have to respect that."

"Of course."

"Thank you for meeting us. We want to apologize for wasting your time."

"It wasn't a waste. I liked you." I hesitated. "Maybe you and I can still be friends."

"I don't think that's a good idea. Take care, Vivien. I hope you find what you're looking for."

"Me too."

I ended the call and put the phone on the floor. I stood there for a while. I got in the bath and slipped underwater and pictured them kissing. Girls were singing.

(B) *editions*

Founded in 2007, CB editions publishes chiefly
short fiction (including work by Gabriel Josipovici,
David Markson and Dai Vaughan) and poetry
(including Andrew Elliott, Beverley Bie Brahic,
Nancy Gaffield, J. O. Morgan, D. Nurkse, Dan
O'Brien). Writers published in translation include
Apollinaire, Andrzej Bursa, Joaquín Giannuzzi,
Gert Hofmann, Agota Kristof and Francis Ponge.

Books can be ordered from www.cbeditions.com.